THE LAND OF ELYON

Into the Mist

THE LAND OF ELYON

Into the Mist

PATRICK CARMAN

SCHOLASTIC INC.
NEW YORK TORONTO LONDON AUCKLAND
SYDNEY MEXICO CITY NEW DELHI HONG KONG

No part of this publication may be reproduced,
stored in a retrieval system, or transmitted in any form
or by any means, electronic, mechanical, photocopying, recording,
or otherwise, without written permission of the publisher.
For information regarding permission, write to Scholastic Inc.,
Attention: Permissions Department, 557 Broadway, New York, NY 10012.

This book was originally published in hardcover by Scholastic Press in 2007.

ISBN 978-0-439-89998-7

12 11 10 9 8 7 6 5 4 3 2 1   11 12 13 14 15 16/0

Printed in the U.S.A.   40
First paperback printing, January 2011

For Christopher Carman,
my Thomas

And with special thanks to
Craig Walker and David Levithan,
who let me wander far and wide

Finding them with open arms on my return
is what made this book possible.

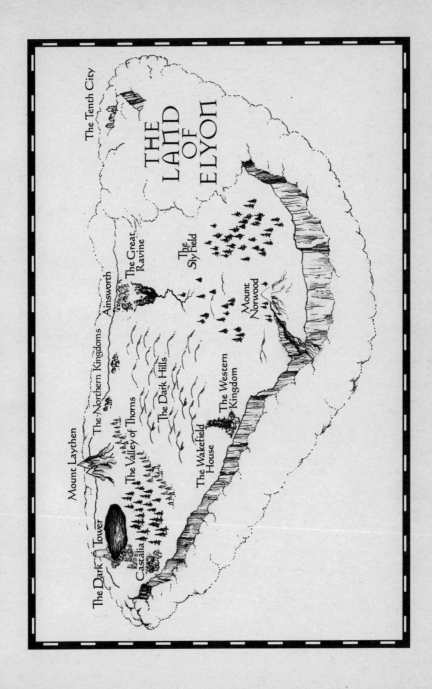

My plans require time and distance.

MARCUS WHITMAN

AUTHOR INTRODUCTION

I have two hopes as I begin telling the tale of *Into the Mist*. The first is that many existing readers have come along for a glimpse into the storied past of two beloved characters: Thomas and Roland Warvold. The second is that *Into the Mist* will introduce new readers to the adventures and mysteries to be had in The Land of Elyon. If you are fulfilling my first hope, then I'm afraid this introduction may be of little use to you — unless of course you've forgotten some or all of what you've already read, in which case I encourage you to read on!

If, on the other hand, you are a reader who is new to The Land of Elyon, this introduction is a perfectly reasonable place to begin.

The first three books in The Land of Elyon series — *The Dark Hills Divide*, *Beyond the Valley of Thorns*, and *The Tenth City* — form a trilogy, chronicling the adventures of a young girl, Alexa Daley, in and around the walled cities of Bridewell Common. When Alexa is able to overcome the walls that surround her, she travels far and wide and discovers a land caught between the forces of good and evil. *Into the Mist* begins shortly after *The Tenth City*, but most of it takes place a generation before Alexa was even born. This was a time when the land was more magical and unstable.

The Land of Elyon is an island with towering cliffs on all sides, and it is here that nearly our entire story occurs. Indeed, the main story of *Into the Mist* takes place within The Land of Elyon, though it begins somewhere else: on the Lonely Sea. At the end of the Elyon trilogy Alexa has left The Land of Elyon on the *Warwick Beacon*, a boat captained by the narrator of *Into the Mist*, Roland Warvold. She has left her home in search of a new adventure, one that she doesn't understand, and it is *Into the Mist* that provides the answer she seeks.

Certain characters and places are introduced in the Elyon trilogy which would be useful for you to be aware of before beginning *Into the Mist*. I offer them as a point of reference, should you become confused at some point in the story. There are dozens of other important characters and places in the lore of Elyon that are not included here, but in truth you need not be concerned with these other details in order to find yourself on a firm footing at the beginning of *Into the Mist*.

Into the Mist will lead you through The Land of Elyon at a time when people were less common in wild places and thus magic roamed more freely. People bring an end to magic, while trees and streams and mountains and animals — left to their own devices — *live and breathe* magic.

Remember this as we begin our journey!

— Patrick Carman
Walla Walla, WA
2006

Characters and places from previous books that intersect with the story of Into the Mist

ALEXA DALEY — The heroine and main character of the Elyon trilogy. At the beginning of *Into the Mist*, she is on the Lonely Sea with her ever-present companion Yipes and the captain of the *Warwick Beacon*, Roland Warvold.

THOMAS AND ROLAND WARVOLD — Adventurous brothers, one by land, one by sea — whose surprising pasts are revealed in *Into the Mist*. **Thomas Warvold** plays a secret role in Alexa's life, revealed in *The Tenth City*. He has also traveled far and wide in The Land of Elyon. **Roland Warvold**, captain of the *Warwick Beacon*, has spent nearly his entire life at sea. He tells the story of *Into the Mist*.

YIPES — A tiny man who once lived on Mount Norwood. Has been in nearly all of Alexa's adventures and continues to be her closest companion.

CASTALIANS — The people who live at the foot of Mount Laythen and are subject to a line of evil rulers. Alexa plays a key role in the rebellion of Castalia and the fight against the tenth of these rulers, known as Grindalls.

ABADDON — The evil force in opposition to Elyon. Elyon is the spiritual force of good in the story, Abaddon the source of all evil.

GRINDALL — A corrupt ancestry of men possessed by Abaddon to do evil in The Land of Elyon.

ANDER — The ruler of the forest in Alexa's time, a grizzly bear. We meet his ancestor, the Forest King, in *Into the Mist*.

THE VALLEY OF THORNS — A dangerous line of defense erected by Victor Grindall's ogres; this vast swath of sharp, poisonous shafts protects Castalia from intruders.

ARMON — The last of the race of giants, onetime keeper of the stones, and friend to Thomas Warvold, Roland Warvold, and Alexa Daley.

ΠOTE:

ALEXA'S CHAPTERS START LIKE THIS.

Roland's chapters start like this.

PART I

THE HOUSE ON THE HILL

One does not discover new lands without consenting to
lose sight of the shore for a very long time.
– André Gide

❧ CHAPTER 1 ❧

A ΠOD
AΠD A WIΠK

There was a chill in the air when I came out from below
and onto the deck of the *Warwick Beacon*. I stood at the
mast alone for a long time and watched soft white mist
swirl on the surface of the water. It's easy to lose track of
time on a long voyage, so it's hard to say how long I stood
there before hearing the sound of footsteps approaching
on the old wooden deck.

"You look well this morning, Alexa."

It was Roland, arriving from the bridge to bring me
my morning cup of tea. He was always up first — before
Yipes or I could imagine raising so much as an eye-
brow — and there was always hot tea to be had from the
captain of the *Warwick Beacon*. It was one of his very few
but frequent indulgences. The tea steamed in the morning
light, and we stood at the rail, no land in sight, the sails
catching a lazy breeze. The cup was warm in my hand, a
comfort against the cold beginning of a new day on the
Lonely Sea.

"Where are we going . . . and when will we get there?"

I had asked both of these questions many times before,
and I'd always received a nod and a wink but no answer. It
had become our morning routine. Roland had long seemed

3

unable or unwilling to share the answers with me, and in this way the day seemed to begin like all the others. Only there was something different this time.

The questions I'd asked hung in the air. He didn't nod or wink or speak, and this made me wonder if the time had come for him to tell me where we were going and when we would arrive.

"We've been out here a long while, haven't we, Alexa?" he began.

"We have," I answered.

"And every morning you ask me the same two questions and get the same response."

I nodded and winked, bringing a smile to my old friend's face.

"I'm all out of nods and winks," said Roland, sipping at his tea. "When Yipes awakens, come find me at the wheel. I'll tell you where we're going. Though you should be warned — it's not a quick or simple thing to share. It will take some time to tell the whole truth."

I handed my teacup back to Roland and raced across the deck to the door leading below. As soon as I threw it open, I began yelling for Yipes and bounding down the steps in search of his tiny hammock. The light from the open door poured into the darkened cabin, but Yipes didn't notice. This didn't surprise me — I had long been certain that if we found ourselves under attack by a loud and angry monster, Yipes would sleep through the entire affair.

4

"Yipes! Wake up! Roland is going to tell us where we're going!"

The belowdecks cabin wasn't very big. There was a small kitchen, a bathroom, and a place to sleep with three hammocks. The three hammocks hung in a row with Roland's first, then mine, then the little one Yipes slept in. It was a good arrangement, since this was the order in which we usually arose in the morning, and it was darkest in the very corner of the room where Yipes hung still and quiet. I yelled the news once more but he didn't move. I hated waking him this way, but we'd been at sea for twenty-five long days with nothing more than twenty-five nods and twenty-five winks. Now there was news to be had, and I was sure he'd want me to wake him for it. I nudged his hammock and let it swing back and forth. Getting no response, I grabbed hold of Yipes's mustache on one side and began to pull. I pulled until his lip was hanging in the air. Then I wiggled his lip all around, but still he wouldn't stir.

I took hold of the hammock from the bottom and flipped it over, dropping Yipes onto the floor of the *Warwick Beacon* with a loud thud. For a moment there was nothing, only the sound of his squashed nose breathing against the wood floor.

"Is that you, Alexa?" came his muffled little voice.

"Yes, it's me! Wake up!"

Yipes slowly sat up, dazed and only half awake.

5

"How did I find my way to the floor?" He rubbed the sleep out of his eyes and twitched his nose. "I was having the strangest dream. It was those two cats from the library — do you remember those wicked cats? They were pulling on my mustache with their sharp teeth. It was awful!"

I wasn't about to tell him who'd really been pulling on his mustache. "Yipes — listen to me," I said.

He was drifting off to sleep again, trying to lie down on the floor, but I took him by the shoulders and shook him fully awake. It struck me once more what a little man he was — like a small child of seven or eight who wished he were bigger. Maybe that was why Yipes was so fond of his mustache, for a mustache was the kind of thing that took all the child right out of a person.

"I asked him where we were going and there was no nod and no wink," I explained.

Yipes shook his head vigorously, rubbed his hands over his face, and looked sternly into my eyes. "No nod and no wink? You're sure of it?"

"I'm sure," I replied.

Yipes jumped to his feet without warning and tangled his head in the hammock. He brushed the hammock away like thick cobwebs until he was free, then together we raced from the cabin into the light of day. The two of us went straight to the bridge in search of Roland and found him standing at the wheel, a cup of tea in one hand and a small nautical journal in the other.

6

We stood before him and waited.

"Hold that, won't you, dear?" Roland held his teacup out to me and I took it from him. "I set your cup over by the stove, in case you should want it."

There was a small wooden door at the center of the wheel that he now opened. It was a part of the wheel that did not turn, and when he opened the door it flopped half-way down and made a flat surface of a size that might accommodate a group of mice having a dinner party. He pulled out an inkwell that had been hidden in the wheel and removed the lid, then took a very old pen from his pocket and tapped the tip twice on his tongue. He inked the pen in the well and began writing carefully in the little book, blowing on the paper now and then to dry his words to the page.

"Tea," he said, and I handed back his cup, which he held along with the pen. He took a drink, then held the cup out once more for me to take. He went back to his writing, occasionally looking out to sea and turning the wheel ever so slightly in one direction or the other.

Yipes poked one of his sharp little elbows into my side, trying to get me to say something, and some of the tea wobbled over the edge of the cup.

"Something on your mind, Yipes?" asked Roland.

"Me? No, not me, sir. I'm only just waking up."

Roland went back to his writing, and I began to wonder if I'd only imagined our earlier encounter. He wasn't a man to be rushed about things, and he practically lived to get the better of Yipes. Trying to find ways with which to make Yipes do silly things seemed to bring endless joy to Roland, our quiet man of the sea. I waited patiently and hoped Roland hadn't changed his mind about answering my questions. He reached his hand out toward me without looking, and I held the cup where he could take hold of it again. He sipped absently, looking out over the sea then back at his notes in the journal before him.

"My tea is cold," he said. Then, looking at my small companion, he added, "Fetch me another cup from the kettle, won't you, Yipes?" Roland took three steps to the very top of the stern and emptied the cold tea over the edge of the boat. "Maybe you could fetch three cups — one for each of us — and when you come back I'll be finished with these notes I'm taking. Maybe then we could have a nice long chat in the chill of the morning."

Yipes beamed and hopped up, taking the cup from Roland and running for the middle of the ship. There was a teapot on a stove set before the entrance to the cabin. The tea was piping hot, and two more cups sat waiting to be filled. I watched from the bridge as Yipes set Roland's cup next to the others and filled all three to the very rim, a terrible habit Yipes could not break and always paid dearly for. As soon as Yipes had all three cups balanced against one another and held firm between his tiny hands as best he could, he began the perilous and slow journey back to the bridge, humming nervously to himself the whole way. Roland smiled as he spun the wheel hard to the right and the wind caught with a snap in the sails overhead. The *Warwick Beacon* pitched into the wind, and Yipes howled as the hot tea spilled over the edges of the three cups.

"He'll never learn," said Roland, turning the wheel back to where it had been.

When Yipes arrived, he was very happy with his effort and didn't seem to mind at all that he'd spilled some of the tea on his hands. He set the cups on the worn wood of the deck and stood straight up.

"Mighty hot tea this morning," he said with a smile. "Mighty hot!"

"It would be best with a bit of morning bread, don't you think?" asked Roland. I took my cup of hot tea in hand and waited while Yipes darted back to the cabin for one of the loaves we'd cooked up the night before. To be fair, I loved to watch Yipes go zinging from place to place on the *Warwick Beacon*. He was very fond of climbing the high masts that held the sails as though they were trees from the forest back home. He would zip from the stern to the bow in the most precarious ways imaginable, never taking the obvious route, and always providing entertainment for both me and Roland.

Roland now smiled at me knowingly, shook the ink from his pen, and began to put his writing things away. By the time Yipes returned with the bread, the little wooden

9

door was shut on the inkwell, the journal and the pen had been pocketed away, and our captain stood silently at the wheel of the *Warwick Beacon*, wisps of gray hair catching on the morning wind.

"Another day, maybe two, and you'll see land once more," he announced.

The answer to my first question had finally come. Twenty-five days on the Lonely Sea would soon come to an end.

Now I repeated my second question. "Where are you taking us, Roland?" I asked. I feared the wink and the nod, that he had changed his mind and would not tell us as we sat holding our warm cups and nibbling at the bread. But I was wrong to fear old Roland would clam up once more, for at last he was ready to take us on an adventure that would last through the day and into the night.

"I have thought a great deal about how to tell you," he began. "It must come in the form of a story — one that finds its beginning when I was near your age. I will tell it just as I remember it, as it happened to my brother and me when we were boys of only ten and eleven."

He looked my way, then off into the sky, as though he were trying to actually see his long-forgotten childhood.

"I do love a good story!" said Yipes, tearing a piece of bread off the loaf with his mouth and wiping the crumbs from his mustache. I held the cup of warm tea close and settled in for a perfect day at sea with my closest friend

10

seated next to me, our shoulders touching to keep warm, and a good long story about to be told.

Roland looked directly into my eyes and moved the wheel ever so slightly.

"We begin with two angry dogs, the boy who owned them, and my brother."

CHAPTER 2

Madame Vickers's House on the Hill

"Get back from there!" The dreadful voice echoing down the stairs into the basement where I slept was familiar. It belonged to a boy named Finch, the son of Madame Vickers, the woman who ran the House on the Hill. As I lay on the dirt floor, I felt a bug crawling along my foot and flicked it away, thinking (as I often did on waking) of the awful situation in which I found myself.

The House on the Hill was the kind of place one might wish on their worst enemy, full of terrible jobs to be done, bad food to be eaten, and regular beatings to be had. I lived there with my brother Thomas because we'd been thrown out of the boys' home in Ainsworth for pulling a wild prank. (A box full of spiders, two snakes, and the headmaster's sleeping wife were all involved.) For years we'd gotten away with such behavior because we'd never been caught, but Thomas had brawled with an older boy and won the day before, and older boys turn to snitching when their status is threatened by someone a year or two beneath them. We were implicated in a series of other similar behaviors and the headmaster's wife — a woman with a near fatal fear of snakes and spiders — insisted my brother and I be gotten rid of.

And so it was that Thomas and I came to Madame Vickers's House on the Hill at the ripe old ages of ten and eleven — myself being ten and Thomas being eleven. The House on the Hill was reserved primarily for children younger than us, children between the ages of six and nine who could be (according to Madame Vickers) "molded into useful laborers." By the time they turned ten they'd be moved off elsewhere to do even more work. Since Thomas and I were the oldest, we were leaders of a band of misfit boys and girls several years our junior, and we prided ourselves on taking care of them as best we could, given the grim conditions.

It's not healthy for a ten-year-old to lie around feeling sorry for himself for too long, especially with young Thomas Warvold in such dire need of help. And so, before I describe more of the House on the Hill, I must get myself out from under my ratty blanket and show how I did my best to free Thomas from Max and the Mooch, the two very large, always hungry, and exceptionally vicious dogs under the care of Finch.

"You think you're funny, do you? I'll show you who's funny!" Finch's voice boomed off the walls and down the stairs once more, and the children around me started to wake.

"It wasn't me! It could have been anyone!"

I ran up the stairs, followed by three or four children who'd been awakened by the racket, and when I reached the top I saw that the dogs had Thomas pinned down in the corner of the kitchen, growling and waiting for Finch to command them to attack. Finch had them each on a twisted old rope of a leash, but they were practically lifting him off his feet as they lunged toward my brother.

"Could you please call off your dogs, Finch?" I didn't yell the question, only spoke it. I'd learned long ago that Finch didn't respond kindly to being told what to do. He was fifteen — a lot older than the rest of us — and generally unwilling to listen to anything we said on our own or as a group. He was especially unfriendly when his mother was not in the house, which was the case on this particular morning.

Finch turned on me and jerked the dogs in my direction, sending me back toward the stairs to the musty old basement. The boys behind me gasped and darted a few steps down the stairs, turning back to the excitement above. They were at that awkward stage in life when curiosity nearly overcame fear, and the two emotions wrestled with each other at times such as these.

"Get back in the basement, or I'll set Max

and the Mooch on you and close the door!" Finch threatened.

The thought of these two monstrous dogs loose in the basement, tearing everything to shreds and quite possibly taking a bite out of more than one child, was more than enough to quiet the group of us. But I had done my job already, for Thomas was not only crafty, he was quick. By the time Finch turned back to the kitchen, the space where Thomas had been was empty. He'd gone out the kitchen window into the open space of the hill.

"Sic 'em, boys!" Finch let Max and the Mooch off the leash and sent them running out the door in search of my brother. He turned to us before leaving.

"The rest of you, back in the basement!"

And we would have done as we were told, too, only it wasn't Thomas standing at the door when the dogs went out, it was Madame Vickers, her icy stare sending a wave of cold energy over the whole house and all that was in it. The moment was frozen and quiet, for the dogs never barked or made mischief when Madame Vickers was present. The only noise they were known to make when they saw her was a quiet whimpering as they waddled off to their beds around the side of the old house with their tails tucked between their legs.

"Finchy," said Madame Vickers, "these boys should be at work by now. They'll need to skip their breakfast and get right to it."

Madame Vickers, like her son Finch, had sharp features — a straight nose that ended in a point far away from the rest of her face, hollow cheeks, thin lips, a long chin. She wore mean-looking boots, made for kicking (or so she said to frighten us), and she had the longest stride of anyone we'd ever seen. It seemed that every step was a yard, meaning that she would often appear before us much faster than we thought possible.

While we stood frozen at the doorway leading to the basement, Madame Vickers turned toward the cart and the horse she'd come in on.

"You there! Out of the cart and into the basement! This boy Roland will show you the way."

A small boy of six or seven emerged from the cart, frightened and in need of a bath. He raced past Madame Vickers and came up short before us.

"Go on then," Madame Vickers ordered. "They won't hurt you. It's me and Finchy you need to worry about." She had the palest skin imaginable, as though she'd never stepped foot outside to feel the warmth of the sun. Everything about her was cold — her voice, her bulging black eyes, and the frozen white skin. It gave kids the chills just to look at Madame Vickers.

She slapped the back of the new boy's head, and he tumbled into the group of us.

"Go back to the basement and get your things," she said, addressing us all at once. From that moment on, the new boy no longer existed as far as our headmistress was concerned. He was one of a throng of boys and girls that held only one purpose for Madame Vickers: "There's money to be made!"

I shooed everyone down the stairs and closed the door, happy at least to have been rid of Finch for the moment and knowing what I would find when the group of us got to the bottom of the stairs.

"This means something good for breakfast!" whispered one of the boys, racing down the stairs with the rest of us following him. The new boy rubbed the back of his head and seemed about to cry, but he hurried down the stairs like the rest of us, wondering what he would find.

When we reached the bottom of the stairs, Thomas was awaiting us, holding out three loaves of bread. We all had hoped he would be there, for there was more than one secret way into the basement from the hill above. As children of the dumping ground, one of our most enjoyable endeavors was to plan and build passageways through the rubble and into the basement. The basement was the one place Madame Vickers would not go. It was dirty

17

and smelly, filled with the stench of unkempt children. She would send Finch on occasion, but for the most part the basement was ours and ours alone.

The breakfast of bread was split into pieces while we dressed and got our burlap sacks for picking garbage. The questions flew at Thomas: *What did you do? Were you scared the Mooch would rip your leg off? How did you get away so fast?* As you may have guessed by now, Thomas was adored by everyone he met. I stood back in the shadows, wondering how long Thomas's luck could hold out. Sooner or later we'd be thrown out of Madame Vickers's House on the Hill too . . . and there was no place else to go.

"Finch is always at the sugar in the kitchen. Have you seen him?" asked Thomas. Everyone nodded and agreed that Finch was notorious for filching spoonfuls of sugar from the bowl. Madame Vickers had been furious just the day before when she'd found the top off the bowl, with some of the sugar missing. It didn't cross her mind to question her beloved Finchy. Instead she set the blame on Thomas — though she couldn't prove it — and gave him a good long thrashing to the bottom with a broomstick.

"I woke early," continued Thomas. Everyone munched on their bread, pulling up their suspenders or buttoning their trousers. "The stairs creak an awful lot, so I used tunnel number two to avoid the dogs. I crept through the kitchen window and took that small sugar bowl – the one Madame Vickers uses at the table when one of the merchants comes from town."

"Get to it, Thomas! We've got to be going," one of the girls said. Everyone was taking a last big bite of bread and hiding scraps under pillows made of old straw and weeds.

"I filled that little sugar bowl and set a spoon right next to it, then I hid in the cupboard and made a bit of a racket. Finch came in all alone, snooping around to find out what was the matter. I cracked open the cupboard a little and watched him notice the sugar bowl on the table. He looked all around, took the spoon, and filled it. Only the thing was, when he put it in his mouth, he coughed and gagged and nearly choked. It was salt I'd put in that sugar bowl, and when he ate it I tumbled out of the cupboard and laughed so hard I couldn't get up!"

"I bet you weren't laughing when he called Max and the Mooch," I added. "You're lucky you got out of there with all your limbs."

Everyone was so proud of Thomas, I didn't have the heart to tell them there would be a price to pay for the missing bread from the kitchen and the salt in the bowl. The trouble with pranks was that someone had

19

to pay, and I was feeling some dread over how much Thomas's morning antics would cost us all.

"No more tricks for a while, okay?" I said as we made our way out of the basement.

Thomas waved me off in his usual way, and I could tell he was already planning some new way of torturing Finch and Madame Vickers.

Madame Vickers's house sat on a dirt hill which had, at one time, been the place where all the trash from Ainsworth was thrown. At some point in its past, the mound of debris began to smell awful enough that the leaders in Ainsworth declared it "officially filled with garbage" and found a new place to get rid of the things they no longer wanted. (The new place they chose was farther away, on the edge of the Dark Hills, where the wind blew steadily away from the town.) The old hill of garbage was covered with a layer of dirt and left to rot.

It was Madame Vickers, working as the disciplinarian of the boys' home in Ainsworth, who hatched the idea to build a house atop the garbage and bring parentless little children there to live. She was paid handsomely for taking these children and training them to do hard labor, removing them from sight so that those in Ainsworth could forget about them. Once a week she returned to Ainsworth with a cart full of trinkets found in the hill of trash to sell or trade, and sometimes she would return with a new boy or girl sitting in the cart where the junk had been. It was a grim introduction for the child to be hauled away like trash from the streets of Ainsworth.

I thought on these things as we made our way down the side of the hill with our itchy burlap bags in tow. Finch was there — tall and skinny as a wire, with greasy hair and a greasy voice — waiting with the dogs who'd gotten their courage back up and were growling at everyone who passed by. Finch could barely control Max and the Mooch when they were leashed, and relied almost entirely on screaming at them and hitting them with a stick in order to keep them from running off or jumping on top of someone.

When Thomas walked by Finch, the older boy gave my brother a nasty look and a tremendous push on the shoulder. Thomas rolled down the hill of garbage but made a game of it, tossing and turning until he landed square on his feet and performed a little dance, finishing with his arms outstretched and all of us cheering.

"You'll be cleaning my unders tonight," Finch sneered. "And the doghouse needs a good scrubbing. How does that sound?"

This took the smile off of Thomas's face and made the rest of us giggle under our breath. There was no worse job than cleaning Finch's undershorts, but cleaning up after the dogs came in close second.

"Get on with it!" yelled Finch, the dogs instinctively growling at his angry voice. "And you best have something worth selling in those bags of yours by midday if you want anything to eat besides a bowl full of salt!"

We worked all day for Madame Vickers, searching the hill of junk for anything we could find that was valuable enough to trade or sell. We found a great many articles of clothing that could be washed and sold to the boys' home or traded in the market. Sometimes we found jewelry, old books with torn pages, broken tools, and chipped dishes. But mostly we discovered only decaying food, old rancid hay from the barns, and things so broken they could never be repaired. It was a good day if you returned with half a sack of junk that might be sold, a bad day if you returned with nothing much and were rewarded with no dinner and a grumbling stomach when the lights were turned out for the night.

It was on that very day — the day on which my story begins — that I found something miraculous. So miraculous was this item that it charted the course of my life and the life of my brother for the rest of our days. It was the very beginning of an unimaginable, lifelong adventure.

CHAPTER 3

At Work on a Hill
of Garbage

Thomas and I moved away from the rest of the group with the new boy in tow.

"What's your name?" Thomas asked. The new boy was small, but his voice was even smaller, as if he'd crawled back into a cave and mumbled out of the darkness.

"Jeremy Jones," he said. "But everyone calls me Jonezy."

"All right, Jonezy it is." Thomas patted him on the back and pointed up the hill. "You see that piece of wood sticking out of the ground? The one with the rag hanging from the end?"

It was a long way off, but Jonezy could see it and nodded.

"Start your first day there," said Thomas. There was a familiar gleam in his eye. "That's a very good spot. You'll find some good clothes that won't need much cleaning up. And you might even find an old ring or two. Madame Vickers loves rings!"

Jonezy smiled in a bashful sort of way and started up the hill while Thomas and I scrambled

23

down a crude path, kicking garbage off to the sides as we went.

"Very clever," I said as we walked.

"What?"

"Hiding things for the new boy," I answered.

"You never know when we'll need a favor. Better the new ones are indebted to us from the start."

Everyone was indebted to Thomas for one thing or another, which I had to admit was a comforting thought as we approached an area we'd been digging at for days. We settled in and began pulling at a block of stone we'd been at the day before, trying to free it from its hold in the stinking mud and filth.

Finch was a ways off at the top of the hill with Max and the Mooch, yelling at some of the other boys to get moving. I looked down the long, wide hill of debris below us and saw for the hundredth time that there was no place to go. The cliffs were near on one side, the Dark Hills went on forever on the other. Way off in the distance was Ainsworth, a city known for its cruelty and meanness toward homeless children. Somewhere far off on the other side of the hill lay the Northern Kingdoms, but I didn't know how far off they were. I looked up at the very top of the hill and could just see the bobbing head of Madame Vickers. She sat in a rocking chair on the wide porch that surrounded the old house. She would sit there all day, eating and drinking what she pleased, waiting for the junk to arrive.

"Roland — look here, I think I've got it loose." Thomas had been busy at the stone while I daydreamed. Now I looked down and saw that he had indeed begun to make some real progress. I knelt down and pulled on the edge of the stone with him, and it started to move with the sucking sound of thick mud. It smelled awful, and we looked at each other with sour faces.

"Maybe we should leave it," I offered. "Whatever we find under there is going to be rotten."

Thomas was undeterred. Once he set his mind to a task — especially one in which some curiosity was to be found — it was impossible to stop him. We heaved on the rock again, and this time a great sucking sound was followed by a loud pop as the stone broke free. We tumbled down the hill and a truly magnificent stench poured forth from the hole where the stone had been.

We looked at each other for a long, silent moment, and then Thomas waved his arms, trying to clear the air, and strode back up the hill. I followed until we reached the stone, which had been turned over. It was crawling with worms and shiny beetles and every kind of creepy insect. The sight of it stopped me in my tracks.

"Take a look at this," said Thomas. There was wonder in his voice, as if he'd found some kind of treasure, but I'd been fooled by him many times before and felt sure he was only trying to trick me now.

"What is it? What's there?"

"Come see for yourself."

I crept very slowly past the rock and stood next to my brother, holding my nose against the thickness of the air.

"I think it's a horse," said Thomas. "It's too big to be a dog."

It certainly was some sort of large animal, or what remained of it, and the more I looked the more convinced I was that it was indeed the remnants of a horse.

"So much for a lost treasure," I muttered, suddenly aware that we'd wasted an awful lot of time digging up something that wouldn't get either of us fed come dinnertime.

"Wait a moment," said Thomas. To my horror he reached down into the space where the decaying horse lay — his hand between the ribs and the squirming bugs — and took hold of something. It was a strap of some sort, made of leather. He pulled mightily on it until his hands slipped free and he nearly fell over backward. The strap did not move,

26

but Thomas was back at it straight away, digging into the soggy muck around the strap.

Not to put too fine a point on the smell of things, but the more Thomas dug, the thicker the air became with the decayed odor of death. I had to turn away in order to keep from getting sick.

"Just leave it, Thomas," I begged, but he wouldn't listen. Before long I was shaking my head but digging with him, trying with all my might to get the thing free so I could convince Thomas to move away from the mess we'd uncovered.

"Okay, step back," said Thomas. We'd managed to claw a lot of mud away from the strap, and Thomas was wiping his hands on his pants, preparing to make another go of yanking what he'd uncovered out of the ground.

"Let me," I said. "I'm stronger than you."

These are the wrong words to use on a big brother, or any brother for that matter. We were virtually the same size, but the fact remained that he *was* a year older, and that meant something in a moment such as this. Thomas looked me up and down, pushed me aside, and grabbed the strap, pulling with all his might. There was a sound of breaking bones as something came free from the ground. Thomas fell back hard, hitting his head against the stone we'd moved. Whatever he had pulled from the earth flew over his head and tumbled down the hill behind us.

When Thomas sat up he was dazed, rubbing his head and looking all around for the object he'd found.

"It's there," I said, pointing down the hill. I could have beaten him to it, but it was he who had been determined to stay at it when I had wanted to walk away. I pulled my brother back up on his feet and followed him toward the object.

"What are you idiots up to now?"

It was Finch coming down without the dogs. He was sometimes like his mother in the way he sneaked quietly from place to place in order to surprise, a wicked habit with only one purpose: to catch someone doing something he or she shouldn't be doing. Lost in our struggle with the strap and the dead horse, we'd forgotten to keep a close eye on him. Finch was quite a bit older and bigger than we were, and he enjoyed pushing us down or punching us in the chest for no particular reason. His fists were clenched as he came, a sign that he was eager to inflict some abuse on both of us.

Finch sniffed the air.

"What's that stench?"

Thomas and I were standing down the hill from the place where we'd uncovered the remains of the horse, but we hadn't yet reached the thing that we'd pulled free. Finch kept walking toward us until he stumbled and slid right into the place where we'd been digging. He sank into the mess we'd uncovered and looked down at his feet. Before he could throw up, he pitched forward and made a heaving sound, but nothing came out. Jumping out of the hole, he ran a few paces back toward the top of the hill, then looked back at us with a growing fury. When Thomas started to laugh, I elbowed him in the side. Finch was in no mood to be ridiculed.

"That's the last time you make a fool out of me!" he screamed. "Just you wait until tonight. We'll see who's so funny!"

I could see that what Finch really wanted to do was to come down the hill and beat the both of us senseless, but the smell was too much for him and his full stomach. He made for the top of the hill, no doubt to tell Madame Vickers of our mischief. My heart sank at the thought of what the rest of the day would bring.

"He thinks we did that on purpose," I said. "We may have accidentally pushed him a little too far this time."

I looked to where Thomas had been standing beside me, but he had moved off, already kneeling by the thing that had been attached to the leather strap. I looked back toward Finch and saw that he was nearing the top of the hill, waving his arms at Madame Vickers.

"Roland, come quick!" shouted Thomas. I darted down the hill and crouched beside him. The strap we'd been pulling on was attached to a grimy old saddlebag with the name Mingleton branded onto it. Thomas had already opened up the bag and put his hand inside. I watched eagerly as he pulled out the one thing that lay hidden in Mingleton's sad-dlebag. It was a single piece of paper — discolored, crumpled, and torn at the edges. But none of that mattered, for we both sat silent and stunned by the worn image and the words on the page before us. A symbol on the paper was something we'd seen before.

We drew our pant legs up and stared at our skinny legs. The symbol on the paper was that of a square and a teardrop put together as one, and the same marking was etched like a tiny birthmark at the top of both our knees. There were more markings on our skin — many more — but of this I will have to tell you later, for just now a bit of trouble had arrived in our midst.

"Give it to me this instant!" We turned our heads to find the bone-white face of Madame Vickers staring down at us, with Finch sneering behind her. The two of them were crafty as cats when they

wanted to be, taking great joy in sneaking up on children who were sitting in the garbage when they ought to be working.

"Give it to me!" repeated Madame Vickers.

Thomas looked as though he was going to make a run for it, and feeling as if it would be a very bad idea if he did, I lurched forward and tore the paper from his hands, holding it out to Madame Vickers.

"Not that, you fool!" She reached her pasty hand down toward us and pointed a long crooked finger at the ground. "That! Give me that!"

I looked at the ground and saw she was pointing to the saddlebag with the name Mingleton on it. Thomas grasped the strap and lifted the bag up toward Madame Vickers. She lurched forward with stunning quickness and seized it. Then she swung it back over her shoulder and belted me clean across the side of the head. The blow laid me flat out on the ground, and through the buzzing noise in my head I heard Finch's rapturous laughter. There was a smear of stinking mud on my cheek, which I tried to wipe away with the back of my hand as I stood up.

"Finchy!" cried Madame Vickers, holding the saddlebag out to him. "Take this and clean it up. It'll fetch a good price at the stables tomorrow." She pointed her awful finger at us again. "And you!"

Madame Vickers was positively outraged. Her eyes seemed about to jump clean out of their sockets and her hands were shaking with nervous energy. She could be very dramatic at times such as these.

"You two have been nothing but trouble since you came here!" she proclaimed. "Come to the thrashing post when the bell tolls. Count the desperate rings of the bell if you have the courage! That's how many lashings you can each expect!"

We thought she was through with us, but there was one last thought on her mind.

"Give me the paper."

I looked at Thomas and he nodded, indicating that I should waste no time handing it over. Both of us were quite convinced that it would take only a moment's hesitation to turn Madame Vickers to violence once more.

Madame Vickers saw what was on the paper and laughed. "There's no hope you'll ever go there, no hope at all. I won't have you daydreaming about some stupid adventure far away from here. That will *never* happen!"

As she turned to go, the paper clutched in her hand, she said to Finch, "Next time bring the dogs and show these filthy boys no mercy."

She turned just one more time in our direction and yelled so loud her voice cracked like a whip on the wind. "Back to work!"

After we were sure they had gone far away, Thomas and I sat down next to each other. We pulled up our pant legs and examined our bare knees, something we'd done a thousand times before. My face felt like it was swollen to twice its normal size, and when I talked, the words came out like a slur.

"Did you see that, Thomas? Did you see what I saw?"

Thomas craned his head around and looked up at Madame Vickers's House on the Hill with a cool smile.

"Our time here has come to an end, brother. But we won't be leaving until the two of them know for certain how rude it is to hit a boy across the head with a saddlebag."

For once I was giddy with excitement at the thought of the tricks Thomas had cooked up to torment Finch and Madame Vickers.

I had a feeling the biggest trick of all was soon to come.

CHAPTER 4

OF KΠEES AΠD MARKİΠGS

I don't think a person has really sat and listened to a very good story in the right way until they've done so with someone like Yipes, someone for whom the real world and the story being told switch places. It's the *Warwick Beacon*, the Lonely Sea, and the man before us who are the story, and the story of the two boys under the rule of Madame Vickers and Finch that is real — so real that one feels the saddlebag against the side of the head, and flies into a rage at the injustice endured by two young brothers.

"That woman!" yelled Yipes. He was beside himself, shaking with anger. "That woman and her terrible son! And those dogs!"

It's hard not to enjoy it when your closest friend is carried away on the wings of a story, and both Roland and I began to laugh. This seemed to bring Yipes back to us, though a glimmer of the House on the Hill remained in his slightly narrowed eyes. He jumped to his feet and gathered the empty cups.

"I'll fetch one more cup of tea for the three of us and another loaf of bread." He started for the stove and then stopped short. "Will you show me your knees when I get back?"

Both Yipes and I held our breath, waiting to see what Roland would say. He made us wait, plying the wheel between his hands, and then he gave us a nod and a wink before Yipes darted off to fill the cups and get the bread.

When he returned, Yipes carefully set the cups on the deck and broke the bread into three pieces. He hunkered down with his cup of tea, blowing off the steam, and I noticed the wind had picked up just a little.

"We should draw down the smaller sail, the one at the very top," said Roland. "We're a bit fast for my taste today."

Yipes shivered from head to toe and his tiny mustache quivered back and forth at the thought of having to wait another second before returning to the story. It took all of his will to set the steaming cup down and stand back up, prepared to do the captain's bidding. He raced across the deck and scampered all the way up the mast until he reached a wooden perch where the topsail could be drawn down.

"Did you really need that little sail taken down?" I asked.

"No, not really," replied Roland. "But I can't help driving him mad at least twice a day. It keeps my spirits up."

Yipes slid down the mast and ran across the deck to rejoin us, careful to avoid the bread and the teacups as he sat back down. He picked up his tea and cradled it gently in his lap, staring intently at Roland's legs behind the wheel of the *Warwick Beacon*.

"Let's see those knees," he said, a twinkle of great expectation in his voice.

It appeared as though Roland thought about whether or not there was another silly errand he could send Yipes on before proceeding, but coming up with nothing very interesting, he decided it was as good a time as any to go on with his story. He stepped out from behind the wheel, locking it with a wooden pin as he came around, and knelt down in front of Yipes and me.

"That piece of paper, the one we found in the saddle-bag," began Roland, looking intently at the two of us, "there was time enough for us to read it before Madame Vickers snatched it away."

"What did it say?" Yipes was about to keel over from anticipation, and the slightest pause from Roland sent him into a fit. "Out with it!"

Roland smiled and, standing just a little, began to roll up his pant legs until they were over his knobby knees. He was quite a burly man, and his legs were covered in a lightly colored mat of furry hair. Yipes and I both leaned in close so we could clearly see his knees.

There appeared to be a very old image directly above his kneecaps. It was dark brown — like a birthmark — but it was also perfect in its shape and form, as if it had been put there by someone. The markings were all of circles, interconnecting and darting back and forth between his knees. Roland touched his knees together and the two halves became one.

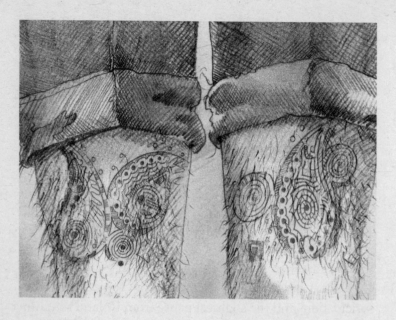

"You've got an awful lot of hair. I can hardly see past it," said Yipes, intent on discovering all he could of the strange markings. He reached his hand down and tried to touch Roland's leg and Roland gave it a quick slap.

"No touching the captain's hairy legs. That's not allowed."

"But what does it mean?" cried Yipes. "All those circles, darting around as if they've got no home."

Roland pulled himself up to his full height and rolled down his pant legs, going back to the wheel. He pulled the wooden pin out and took control of the *Warwick Beacon* again.

"Thomas had markings on his legs as well," he said.

"Only his were all squares. If we sat across from each other when we were young, all the squares and all the circles became connected. We looked at it for years, trying to understand what the markings meant and from where they had come, but we could never figure it out."

Roland paused, taking one of his hands from the wheel and scratching at his ear.

"Until we found that piece of paper at Madame Vickers's House on the Hill."

Yipes and I looked at each other with wide eyes, feeling sure we were about to be let in on a fantastic secret. We watched as Roland took his logbook out of his pocket and opened it to a certain page. He handed the book over — something he'd never done before — and Yipes quickly reached out and snatched it away.

"Careful with that!" cried Roland. "If it goes over-board we won't know where we're going or how to get back."

Yipes was suddenly aware that he had in his hands a very important item that he didn't care to be responsible for. He thrust it into my hands and leaned in close, where the two of us spied a drawing on the left-hand page.

"As close as I can recall, that is a reproduction of the piece of paper we found in the Mingleton's saddlebag at the House on the Hill," said Roland, gazing off into the horizon.

Yipes and I looked carefully at the page, reading the words and spying the image of the square and the circle

WESTERN KINGDOM
WAKEFIELD HOUSE

FAILED!

Miss Flannery
Miss Flannery

put together. It was uncannily like the one we'd just seen on Roland's knee.

"If you want to know the meaning of those words and that image before the sun sets, we best get back to our story," said Roland. "Take up your bread and your tea and I'll tell you what happened that night at Madame Vickers's House on the Hill."

CHAPTER 5

The Toll of the Bell

For the rest of the day Finch kept the dogs on their long leashes and let them stray between the piles of trash. He set us all to picking through the same giant stretch of rubbish, where he could keep a watchful eye and sic Max and the Mooch on any-one who slacked off. There was nothing in the world like the thought of two very big, very mangy dogs tearing at your ankles to make a boy work faster.

Thomas and I whispered of a great many things as the day passed. We whispered of the symbol on our knees and how it had matched that of the image on the piece of paper from the saddlebag. We won-dered aloud what the words on the piece of paper had meant — *Western Kingdom* — *Wakefield House* — *Miss Flannery* — *FAILED!* We wished we could have the paper back again, to try to find something else written there that might enlighten our search for answers. We also spent a good deal of time talking about the bell that would soon toll and how we needed to escape what was likely to be the beating of our lives. On this topic Thomas was the primary planner, having spent hours and hours thinking

41

about what he might do to Madame Vickers and Finch should we ever find a way to leave the House on the Hill for good.

"One thing is for sure," I said after some thought. "We simply have to go to the Western Kingdom, by whatever way possible, and seek out the Wakefield House and Miss Flannery."

On this point we agreed, and soon we were planning our escape in hopes of making our departure before the sound of the bell drifted over the hill of garbage. Throughout the morning, Thomas secretly darted back and forth between the younger children, calling in every favor he'd saved up for just such a time as this. Our stomachs rumbled as the noon hour approached and the dogs became excited as Madame Vickers strode down the winding path with two bags slung over her shoulder and a dirty old jug in her hand.

When she arrived, she stared boldly at the group of us and seemed to take some pleasure in tossing one of the bags in our general direction. The bag burst open when it hit the ground, revealing a block of moldy cheese and two loaves of hard, stale bread. Max and the Mooch bolted forward, yanking their leashes from Finch's hand, and pounced on the food. They began by tearing the cheese to pieces, making such an awful sound of growling and slobbering and chomping that not one of us had even a tenth of the courage it would have taken to reach in and try our luck at grabbing something for ourselves. When all the cheese was gone, each of the dogs chomped down on a loaf of bread and, growling viciously in our direction for good measure, returned to lie down by Finch and eat the rest of our lunch.

"Next time you'll need to be quicker," Madame Vickers said with a sly grin, as though she'd been imagining the scene that had just taken place and was glad to find it playing out as she'd hoped. "I suppose now you'll have to go without food until dinner."

She turned to Finch and handed him the other bag and the jug she'd carried down the hill. We all watched him open the bag and take out a fresh loaf of bread, a glorious-looking red apple, and slices of delectable-looking orange cheese. "Enjoy your lunch, Finchy. And do keep a close eye on *that* one." She pointed at Thomas. "Who knows what he'll try next!"

She started up the hill, then yelled back over her shoulder, "Give them the jug when you've had all you want. They'll work faster if they're not too thirsty."

Finch nodded and took a bite of the apple, savoring the crunchy sweetness. None of us moved as the dogs choked down the last of our bread and

Finch guzzled from the jug. When Madame Vickers had gone far enough up the hill that she could not hear Finch any longer, he looked us up and down where we stood and took another bite of the apple.

"Back to work with you!" he screamed, sputtering apple juice down his chin and wiping it with a grimy arm. "The next one of you fools to find something of real value gets the core of this apple. But it must be small enough to fit in my pocket. A ring or a coin will do just fine."

He went on eating the apple, and Thomas moved closer to the new boy, Jonezy, as if to secretly whisper to him. Jonezy was smaller than the rest, too frail to be working on a hill of garbage all day without food or water. He had been quiet and seemed to be afraid of the other boys, though no one had bothered him.

Thomas reached down into one of his own mismatched shoes, a shoe of brown leather found on the hill. He dug around the edge of the shoe, which was easy for him to do, because the shoe was several sizes too big and there was lots of room to get his fingers in along the sides. When his hand emerged there was an old silver coin between his fingers.

"Have you got anything good yet?" asked Thomas. The boy dug nervously into his bag and pulled out a twisted piece of metal, the spine of a book with no pages inside, and a ring with prongs bent wildly where some sort of stone used to be. He held the objects out for Thomas to see, and Thomas nodded as though he was impressed. The boy smiled and began putting the things back in the bag. It was then that Thomas did the kind of thing that made me very proud to be his brother, the kind of thing he did all his life. While Jonezy was turned away, Thomas flicked the coin into the dirt where the boy had been working and then he walked the three steps back to where I was picking at my own little place in the trash. I wasn't the only boy who saw the scene unfold, nor was I the only one who smiled when the new boy held up the treasure, unable to contain his excitement.

"I've found a coin!"

It was the first time he'd made so much as a sound barely above a whisper, and we found that when he wanted to, he had quite a good set of lungs on him.

Finch looked up with a mouth full of gooey cheese and waved the boy over. He put out his grimy palm, and the boy handed over the coin. Finch rubbed the coin with his thumb and asked, "What's your name?"

"My name is Jonezy. I found that coin, just there in the dirt." Jonezy pointed to the place he'd been working.

Finch took what was left of the apple in his hand and tossed it over Jonezy's head, where it skidded in the dirt, turning the beautiful white of the bites that remained brown and dirty. The dogs were both in a panic to get at the treat, but Finch held them back this time.

"There you are, Jonezy. Best pick it up quickly or I'll let the dogs at it."

Jonezy raced back to the apple, wiped it three or four times on his shirt, and chomped every part of it down in two big bites.

When Finch was finished with his lunch, he followed his mother's instructions and gave the jug to us. Then he sat down with the dogs and examined the coin. With afternoon approaching, there was still no sound from the bell. Madame Vickers was making us wait in order to heighten our anxiety. A shame for her, since it allowed us the time we needed to devise plans of our own, time that Thomas and I used to our advantage as we secretly plotted amongst ourselves.

As late afternoon turned to the dinner hour, we began the long walk up the hill with our burlap bags thrown over our shoulders. Finch took up the rear, using the dogs to herd us like cattle up the side of the mountain of garbage. The bell still had not rung, but upon seeing the lot of us making our way up to the House on the Hill for whatever food we could

46

hope for, the shadowy figure of Madame Vickers appeared at the thrashing post with a mallet in her bony hand. She banged the bell that hung on the porch, the start of what felt like a funeral march of children up the gloomy hill. We were still a long way off when the bell had rung twenty times. No one had ever endured more than twenty lashes, and there was no telling how high the number would go.

"You picked the right time to get away from here," came a voice from one of the young girls ahead in the line. "I wish we could come with you."

Thomas surprised me then, for he made her an offer we hadn't discussed.

"If we find a better place than this — a safer place — we'll come back for you."

All of the dirty little faces in the line ahead of us turned and looked at Thomas. He'd given them hope, and this seemed to me like a reckless act. I turned away from the small faces before me, knowing the odds of our heroic return to rescue a group of boys and girls from a hopeless future were slim.

I looked up, and the bell kept ringing. Madame Vickers just stood there and banged it over and over again. Could she really mean to thrash us so many times?

As we approached the last turn on the path of

smashed debris leading up to the House on the Hill, Thomas set our plan in motion. He was at the very back of the line with only Finch and the dogs trailing a ways behind. Finch was absentmindedly kicking at the garbage at his feet when Thomas tapped me twice on the shoulder. I shuddered to think what would come next. I tapped the girl in front of me twice, and on it went up the line to the very front, until the very last boy – Jonezy – was tapped, and he ran screaming off the path into a sea of trash before him.

"Get back here!" yelled Finch from somewhere behind us, suddenly aware that one of the children in his charge had bolted from the line. The bell finally stopped at thirty-eight (I had counted every one) as Madame Vickers watched the boy race off yelling and pointing.

"Sic the dogs on him!" shouted Madame Vickers from the porch. She was still far off, but the boom of her voice carried over us to Finch and he let loose Max and the Mooch. He followed after them, and the rest of the boys and girls pulled back in a group, providing just enough cover for me and Thomas to duck down low and crawl back down the hill. We didn't go very far – only back around the one corner – until we came to a place that had been there for a long time, a secret place hidden in the debris. Around the corner and in a crevice of junk sat the stump of a tree, its twisted roots exposed and shooting out like a blanket of thick snakes. We had long before dug out a big hole next to the stump, then moved the stump to cover the hole. It was our secret place, where we hid certain things we found but did not give to Madame Vickers.

"Grab hold!" said Thomas.

We each took a large root in our hands and heaved one side of the stump up in the air. I was first to go under, then Thomas pushed the trunk up as hard as he could and dove beneath it. The stump crashed down and caught one of my legs, but we were hidden beneath the roots of the tree where no one could see us.

Whether or not we were safe was a completely different matter.

CHAPTER 6

My Shoe Goes Missing

Tiny shards of light made their way through the tangle of weeds and dead roots so I could see Thomas sitting quietly amongst the junk we'd collected over time. The hole we'd dug out under the stump was like a buried treasure chest filled with the most useful artifacts we'd found in the mountain of garbage, things we'd been unwilling to hand over so that Madame Vickers could use them to trade in the town that had forgotten us. We stayed very still, watching the dust settle through the soft light, listening for the sound of Finch and the dogs.

I was lying on my back with my leg propped up over my head. I could see only as far as my knee. The lower half of my leg and my foot were wedged between the ground and the twisting knot of roots. There was a sharp rock poking into my shin, and it was beginning to send a sharp pain up my leg.

"Thomas," I whispered, "I don't hear anyone. Can you push the trunk up so I can free my leg?"

Thomas put his finger to his lips, cautioning me to remain silent. I heard only the distant sound of boys and girls hollering, so I scowled at my brother and tried to free my leg by wiggling it back and forth. This, I realized too late, was a mistake. Dirt clods and rocks poured down my pants, and a poof of dust filled the air, and still my leg remained tangled in the roots of the tree. I was no closer to freeing myself, and the sharp rock was wedged even more painfully into my leg than it had been. To make matters much worse, Thomas had always been prone to sneezing and coughing when the wind had kicked up too much dust on the hill, and I could see in the whites of his eyes and his shaking head that he was about to let loose with a tremendous assortment of sounds. First he coughed lightly, trying to hide the sound in his cupped hands, which only served to enlarge the volume into a soft echo through the hole under the stump. He began sniffing, then cleared his throat. Unfortunately, these sounds were the beginning of a much louder measure in the symphony of his reaction to the dirty air in the closed space. Next came the coughing, soft at first but growing louder, then an explosive sneeze. He finished by clearing his throat once more and spitting into the dirt. Then he looked at me.

"Please don't do that again," he whispered, running his arm across his nose and sniffing softly while I did my best to keep completely still.

"It seems to have worked," I offered, trying to make him feel better. The idea had been to send one of the boys running off the path until Finch and the dogs caught up. Thomas had provided a very handsome inkwell that could be cleaned up and sold along with a matching pen that was cracked down one side but otherwise perfectly usable. These were to be produced when Finch arrived, as though they had been spotted from far off and had to be snatched right away. The risk for the boy who chose the task was that of being attacked by Max and the Mooch, but Jonezy was the first to volunteer, which seemed actually to make the most sense. He was the only one among them that would reasonably be willing to run off the path in search of some object with Max and the Mooch right behind him. He didn't know the danger of his actions, for he hadn't had the experience of being chased by two large dogs.

"I didn't hear any screaming," I continued. "So the dogs probably didn't attack Jonezy. They just scared him, like they sometimes do."

It was true the dogs were sometimes more bark than bite, but I could see that Thomas was concerned for Jonezy, and we both felt a heavy guilt for having quite literally thrown him to the dogs on his very first day at Madame Vickers's House on the Hill. We hadn't imagined Finch would let the dogs attack the boy.

Our concern over Jonezy's well-being was soon

overshadowed by the sound of voices nearing the stump.

"I tell you they've heard something." It was Finch, still a ways off but getting closer.

"Take the dogs and find them," came the shrill sound of Madame Vickers. "Don't hesitate to sic the dogs on them if they run. They must be found and punished!"

I could hear Max and the Mooch crying as if they were pulling hard, their collars tightening around their thick necks as they leaned toward the stump. It was frightening to think of Finch removing the stump and letting the dogs at us there in the hole where we could not escape.

"Go find 'em! Go on now!" Finch had let the dogs off their leashes. They seemed to be darting every which way, but at least one of them was getting closer. I looked at Thomas and saw that he was having trouble holding back a cough or a sneeze, I wasn't sure which. He sniffed quietly, concentrating all of his energy on trying to suppress whatever noise was trying to escape from his throat.

"I'm all right! Wherever you've gone off to, I'm all right!" It was the unmistakable high voice of Jonezy, far away but clear. I glanced over and saw Thomas smiling in the small light, but he only smiled for a moment, for the sound of a dog came nearer. Max and the Mooch had separated, and now one of them was growling at the roots near my foot. My breathing shook with fear as I thought of my foot, hoping it wasn't right out in the open where the dog could take hold of it.

I was now sure it was the Mooch by the sound of his growling. It was widely agreed by all the boys and girls at Madame Vickers's house that if you had to be locked in a room with either Max or the Mooch it would be considerably worse if you were stuck with the Mooch. The Mooch was the more aggressive of the two — the more likely to strike without thinking — and he was also bigger.

The Mooch was growling and digging around my foot, and then to my horror he seemed to have gotten ahold of the sole of my old shoe. He was yanking hard, pulling back on his haunches in violent jerks.

"Mooooooooch?" Finch's voice cracked through the air like a long whip as he searched for the dog. The Mooch gave one last ferocious pull on the shoe, and it came off in his mouth. Something about the idea of having this murderous dog's teeth wrapped around my bare foot made me fight with everything I had in me to get my foot down inside the hole where it would safe. I felt the sharp rock scrape hard against bone and the gnarly roots grab at my bare skin as my leg came free.

"Mooch!" Finch cried again, this time with more

anger in his voice, as though he were planning to kick the dog the moment he saw him. I clenched my teeth against the pain in my leg and listened as the Mooch tore off toward his master, my shoe wedged firmly in its mouth.

"You come when I call you and not a second later!" Finch was lecturing the dog as though it could understand him, and to my astonishment it sounded as though he and the Mooch were moving off in the other direction.

"And stop picking up junk! I'm not throwing any shoes for you to fetch until we find those boys."

We could hear the Mooch whimpering as they drifted down a different path toward the bottom of the hill. The dust settled in the hole and our eyes had grown used to the light. For the moment, we were safe.

"Better your shoe than one of your toes," said my brother. "He would have chewed that big one right off without thinking twice."

We both knew this was more fact than fiction, and maybe that was why we laughed so hard at the thought of the Mooch running around the hill with my big toe hanging out of his mouth. It wasn't even funny, when you really thought about it, but the nervous energy in our small space needed to get out, and boys will be boys when it comes to what we think is grounds for a good laugh.

"How bad does that hurt?" asked Thomas, staring wildly at the gash running down my leg.

"Pretty bad," I offered, rolling down my pant leg to cover the wound so I could begin forgetting about it. "What do we have for shoes down here?"

We sat in the middle of the hole, but we had dug a sort of cave on one side that held our treasure of found objects. Within that treasure were extra shoes of a size that fit one or the other of us. Thomas picked up the best of the bunch.

"Try this one," he said. I did, and found that it was too small. Thomas looked sideways at it, removed his own left shoe, and replaced it with the one he'd offered me.

"How about this one?" He held up a black boot that couldn't have been a worse match to the brown shoe I was already wearing. But it fit perfectly and I wasn't in a position to be picky about color or style in the things I wore on my feet. We were apt to have a long night ahead of us, and good traveling shoes were essential. The black boot would do just fine.

When I looked back, Thomas had his hand back in the hole where all the things we'd kept were hidden. He pulled out a small wooden box of a size that would fit in his pocket, which I'd seen many times before. The box sat atop his most prized possession, a journal he'd stolen from the House on the

Hill. It had created quite a stir when the new journal — at the time filled with only blank pages — had gone missing from Madame Vickers's study. But Thomas was never caught with it and only showed it to me after the news of its disappearance had died down. He cherished every page, taking great care to use every square inch of space. I often saw him counting the blank pages that remained, so that he would know how many more paintings he could do before the journal was full. Thomas was extraordinarily gifted at painting pictures, and he loved to paint them whenever he could sneak away. He could draw something as big as Madame Vickers's house in great detail within the space of a few inches, such was his desire to paint everything he could while using the least amount of space in the journal.

The little wooden box he held contained the things he needed to make the paintings. He was fond of cutting bits of soft hair from all the children's heads. He found small sticks that fit his hand the way he liked, and made pasty white glue by mixing water with wheat flour and alum he stole from the kitchen. In this way he made crude brushes from the sticks, the glue, and the children's hair. His little wooden box also contained a dozen or more tiny pouches he'd made from old clothes and drawstrings found on the hill. One of the pouches was filled with hair, another contained a mix of dry flour and alum, and the rest were filled with colored powders of his own making. His color palette was surprisingly varied, for he had a way with mixing powdery red stone, dried wild flowers of every color, and burned black soot that gave him a rainbow of opportunity within the small cloth bags. He always mixed his powdery colors with his own saliva – never water – declaring that it made the images more personal, and he only used brushes made of hair from the children's heads, for he felt it infused his work with the powerful combination of sadness and vibrancy of those he loved.

For now Thomas tucked the small treasures safely away in his pockets, but we'd need more than a little wooden box and a journal to escape the House on the Hill.

"What else have we got in there that we can use?"

Thomas sniffed – his nose was still running from the dust – and he responded, "Well, there's no food, but there's some rope, two rusty knives, a flint and steel so we can make a fire when we want, three old candles. . . ." He trailed off as he kept digging into the pile. I stayed quiet and rubbed my leg, wondering how in the world we were going to survive with such meager supplies.

"There's a bag here we could throw over a shoulder, and I think it'll hold everything. And here's an old jug, but there's nothing in it." He popped the cork on the jug and turned it upside down. Nothing came out.

While we were looking through the things we'd saved up, I started thinking it wasn't quite as good a collection of treasures as I'd once thought it was. It was depressing to think that these were the best things we'd been able to save in all our digging through mound after mound of trash.

My self-pity in the hole under the tree stump was interrupted by the distant sound of Madame Vickers screaming from the porch of the house.

"There's no place to run where I won't find you!"

Thomas and I both froze in the hole at the cold sound of her words.

"Everyone knows where you belong! There's no town that won't ship you right back to my front door, and when they do . . ." She seemed to hang on those words, to make us wonder what she would say. "Those clangs of the bell will still be here waiting for you. And worse! Much worse punishment than that!"

I stared at the floor of the hole, not sure what to do.

"Maybe we should turn ourselves in," I said hesitantly. "Take our beating and maybe even get something to eat." I hadn't eaten all day and was very hungry.

Thomas could see that I was rapidly losing courage. He reached back into the place where he'd been pulling things out and produced a cloth bag that was tied at the top. When he opened it and laid the cloth out flat on the ground between us, there were dozens of coins, rings, necklaces, and medallions lying there. They'd even been polished up some so that it really did look like a bag of treasures, things that we might actually be able to trade for food or water. I hadn't known he'd been hiding such things.

"These will take us a long way," said Thomas. "Maybe as far as we need to go."

Then he yanked up both his pant legs. I hiked up mine as well and we sat in the dim light of the hole, looking at the strange markings on our knees, thinking of the piece of paper we'd found, and knowing in our hearts that we had to leave Madame Vickers's House on the Hill and find the Wakefield House.

❧CHAPTER 7❧

Avalanche!

Night had come to the hill several hours before, and still we waited. We held out some hope that one of the other children would bring us something to carry along with us — some food or water or both — and that we might hear some news of what Madame Vickers and Finch were up to. The time passed slowly in such tight quarters, and we whispered our plans until sometime deep in the night I drifted off to sleep.

I don't know how long I sat sleeping, but suddenly there was a finger poking into my ribs and I jerked awake, thinking of the Mooch and hoping he hadn't gotten ahold of me in the night.

"Wake up," Thomas said. "Someone's coming."

I was alert at once, listening carefully, hoping not to hear any growling or barking. For a moment it was quiet, only the sound of a soft breeze blowing in from the Lonely Sea — but then we heard a tiny voice from the outside.

"Thomas? Roland? Are you in there?"

Thomas was on his feet in a flash, pushing up on the stump and beckoning me to help. Two boys were outside. Their names were Philip and Henry, and they struggled to hold up the old roots as we scampered out, all of our possessions in the one bag thrown over my shoulder.

"I thought you'd never come," said Thomas. "Where are the dogs?"

"They're chained up in the usual place," said Henry, the smaller of the two boys. "We thought Finch would stay up forever, but he finally fell asleep in the chair on the porch."

"And Madame Vickers?" I asked, certain that she was watching the four of us and would come around a corner at any moment.

"She's gone," said Philip. "Left hours ago with the horse and the cart. My guess is she went to tell everyone in Ainsworth about you two. Maybe she even doubled back to the north. You better be careful who you trust."

"Did you bring anything?" asked Thomas.

Henry held out a sack. "There's not much — a little bread and half an apple, a few nuts, and a bottle of water. That's all we had hid in the basement, and there's no getting at the kitchen tonight. They have it locked down tight."

There was an awkward silence on the hill as the boy handed over the paltry bag of rations. It wouldn't last a day — in fact, it would probably be gone before we reached the bottom of the hill — and it was not the way in which my brother and I had hoped to get our start.

"Where will you go?" asked Philip, a look of genuine concern on his face. "You can't go into town or to the sea, and there's nobody stupid enough to go into the Dark Hills. I'd sooner stay under the stump than go that way."

I looked at Thomas, but he seemed unwilling to give away our plans. Maybe he knew, as I didn't, that Madame Vickers would question the boys mercilessly. Better that they really didn't know where we'd gone and why.

"What's that sound?" asked Thomas, always the most perceptive in a group of any size.

"I don't hear anything," said Philip.

"You'd better get back by the secret way and quick," said Thomas. "Don't wake Finch, and stay clear of those dogs."

The boys looked at each other and nodded, then started back up the hill. Henry turned back for a final word. "Don't forget what you said, about coming back for us if you find a better place."

Thomas waved them off in the moonlight, and the two boys raced up the hill toward Madame Vickers's house. When their footsteps could be heard no more and we felt certain they were safely in the basement, I turned to Thomas.

"Are you ready?" I asked.

"I am, but we'll need to swing wide. Madame Vickers is coming this way."

A shiver ran through me as I thought of her in the cart, moving toward the house with the horse before her. It was then that I heard the clomping of faraway hooves and knew that she had indeed returned and would soon come up the hill toward us.

We veered away from the noise, toward the Lonely Sea, to a place where there was no path and the way down was steep and dangerous. Slowly we crisscrossed down the side of a mountain of debris until we came near the bottom in the dead of night. I became careless when I could see the bottom of the hill and went more quickly than I should have, which started a very small garbage avalanche. But the small problem became much bigger when the avalanche I'd caused met with Thomas's feet, for he was in front of me as we went. His feet slid out from under him, and he began sliding down the hill. I jumped into the fray of moving junk to try to rescue him, and the two of us went head over heels down the side of a hill that was now sliding out from under us, making a tremendous racket that no two dogs within a mile could have slept through.

Sure enough, as we tumbled down the hill, we could both hear the distant echo of Max and the Mooch barking. We toppled along the hill, hollering as we went, bouncing off sharp and hard objects alike until we slammed into the bottom. A wave of descending garbage threatened to cover us. We scrambled to our feet, out from under the onslaught of an avalanche that sparked and flew as it hit the bottom of the hill. As quickly as we could, we ran and ran toward the cliffs that dropped off to the Lonely Sea.

"Hold up!" I yelled to Thomas after a time. "You don't want to run right off the edge, do you?"

Thomas pulled up, and we both tried to catch our breath. We were tired and scraped up, scared half to death, and we hadn't eaten anything all day.

"Give me that water bottle," said Thomas. "My mouth is so dry I can hardly swallow."

I dropped the bag to the ground and opened it up, taking out the bottle of water. It was lucky for both of us that it hadn't broken on the way down. I took out the cork and handed the bottle to Thomas, then watched him drink down half of it. He coughed and sputtered, handing it back and gesturing that I should finish it off. When I was through, I tossed the bottle aside, knowing we had a wooden jug in the bag that would work better if we lived long enough to find water again.

As we calmed down and our breathing slowed, we both heard the sound of Max and the Mooch from far away. Looking up the hill, we saw firelight snaking down the main path. There were two lights, one bobbing up and down as though the person under it were running, the other steadier and well out in front. It was Madame Vickers, racing down the hill in her horse-drawn cart with a torch in hand, and Finch in hot pursuit with the dogs.

"This is bad," I said. "Very bad."

Thomas smiled wryly in the moonlight, as if he expected some miracle to save us.

"Maybe not quite as terrible as it looks," he said. "You forget how many favors I was owed."

As if on cue, there came a crashing sound from somewhere up on the hill. It was hard to see exactly what was going on in the night, but the bobbing torch carried by Finch sped up, then abruptly stopped, the dogs barking incessantly and the sound of Finch's voice screaming at them to shut up.

"I was beginning to wonder when it would come off," said Thomas.

"What do you mean?" I asked him.

Thomas smiled, still catching his breath.

"One should never go whipping around sharp turns in a wooden cart without checking to make sure all the wheels are on tight. Don't you think?"

We laughed at the thought of Madame Vickers lying in the garbage and hoped she'd landed in a stinky mud hole full of the nastiest stuff from the hill. We only stayed a moment, listening to the mottled sound of Finch and Madame Vickers cursing and screaming. Then Thomas grabbed the bag and we started running toward the city of Ainsworth.

"They won't give up so easily," I said as we ran.

"You're probably right," offered Thomas. "Which is why we should keep running until we get to the city. If we can make it there ahead of Max and the Mooch, I think we can lose them in the winding streets."

Going back to Ainsworth worried me. It would be best if we could pass through quickly – selling some of our treasure of trash for food and water – and be away before morning.

CHAPTER 8

A Dark Night
in Gaul's Ward

The sound of the dogs grew nearer as the night wore on, for though Thomas and I were fast on our feet, we were no match for a much older boy being ruthlessly pulled along by Max and the Mooch. The city of Ainsworth was an hour away at a dead run, which we couldn't keep up without resting every five minutes or so. We would be lucky to make it all the way in an hour and a half, and Finch was gaining on us as the distant lights of Ainsworth came into view.

We stopped short of the city itself, trying to catch our breath, knowing full well that we would have to sneak in without being seen. It was likely Madame Vickers had already visited while we had waited under the stump on the hill, telling the authorities to be on the watch for two young boys who'd escaped her grasp. They would be looking for us from the very direction we were coming.

"I'm not sure how we'll get in without being seen," said Thomas. It struck me then that he had no idea how we were to proceed. He had thought only of getting us out of Madame Vickers's clutches, not of the difficult tasks that lay ahead.

"There's one place we could probably get in," I said. "And it's probably the best place to trade what we have for the things we'll need if we're to make it all the way to the Western Kingdom."

To be fair, we had no idea where the Western Kingdom was. We only knew it was a long way off and to the west, through places hardly anyone had ever been, and that without at least some supplies we had no hope of making it.

The dogs were closing in, and we could see Finch's torch dancing over his head.

"I see you! I see you! Get back here or I'll let loose the dogs!" Finch was yelling at the top of his lungs, and we realized we'd let him get too close. If he did let the dogs go, they might overtake us before we could reach the edge of Ainsworth and get in.

"Follow me!" I said, and we were off toward the edge of the city at a full sprint. When we came near enough to see the buildings and the streets of the city, we veered quickly to the left and ran along the outer edge in the dark. No one could see us in the night, and no one would expect us to enter at the place I'd chosen. We ran with everything we had in us, as Finch's voice boomed, *"Go get 'em! Go get 'em!"*

He had let Max and the Mooch off their leashes.

"Here, Thomas!" I pointed toward Ainsworth and turned sharply in the direction of dim lights.

"You're crazy!" he said, but we both kept running.

"There's no other way in without being seen!"

The Mooch advanced within a few yards of us. He'd moved out past Max and was closing in on me, growling as though he'd come within range of a victim he could devour. He needed only to charge a few more feet to do it.

Thomas reached the surrounding fence before me, scampering up the side. He looked back, and by the dim light of the streetlamps I saw in his expression that the Mooch was about to take hold of me by the leg. With a final burst of effort, my lungs stinging with pain, I leaped into the air and seized the top of the fence, kicking to reach the top. The Mooch stood up on his back legs and clamped his mighty teeth into my new black boot.

"Not this time! That boot belongs to me," I said. Turning my body in midair, I kicked the Mooch square in the ear with my free foot. He yelped in pain as Max came alongside him, and the two dogs barked angrily at the base of the fence. Reaching the top, I pushed Thomas over the edge and jumped down beside him, where we lay in a heap on the ground.

And so it was that we entered Ainsworth by a very dangerous way, a way not intended for children. And worse, the sound of the dogs had alerted someone. We were not alone on the other side of the fence.

"Well," came a slippery voice over the sound of the dogs, "what have we here?"

We were in the worst part of Ainsworth, the slum of all slums, and there was a big man with greasy hair and a tangled beard standing before us. He took us both by the backs of our shirts and hauled us up on our feet, forcing us down a darkened alley with hands so big I thought they couldn't be real.

"Word's on the street about you two," he muttered. "I'm pleased you've come my way."

He laughed thunderously, as though he couldn't have cared less who knew he was dragging two innocent boys down a dirty street. I tripped and started to fall, and the man's big hands lifted me clear off the ground by my shirt and set me to walking again. In that moment I glanced back and saw Finch staring over the fence with a look of amusement on his face. He knew, as I did, that Thomas and I were in the biggest trouble of our young lives.

We had come upon Gaul's Ward with only an hour of night remaining. A cool mist hovered in the alleyway and a strong smell of rotting vegetables stung my nose as I tried to catch my breath. There was trash strewn everywhere on the cobbled streets as we walked past crisscrossing alleyways and broken-down houses. Gaul's Ward was the place you went if you had no money and no prospects, and it was not a place you ventured into alone or at night. It was sheer madness to come here if you were a child, for children were known to disappear into Gaul's Ward all the time, never to be seen or heard from again.

"Where are you taking us?" asked Thomas, usually the bolder of the two of us in times such as these.

"Where Madame Vickers won't find you," the man growled. We couldn't be sure if he wanted to hide us so that we could become his slaves or because he truly did want to protect us from being found.

"How far is it?" Thomas continued with the questions, which clearly annoyed the man who had us in his grasp.

"Keep quiet!" he answered with a firm and booming voice.

The more we walked, the fewer lamps there

were, the darker the alley became, and the more rats I saw darting back and forth before my feet in the shadows and mist. We came to a set of stairs that led down into the darkness. Only the first three steps could be seen; the rest were shrouded in mist and deathly quiet.

I craned my neck to the side so I could look back down the alley from which we'd come. Through the swirling mist I saw the inhuman strides of Madame Vickers and heard the clomp of each boot on the grimy cobblestones before her. She looked positively wicked in the dim light, like a monster coming through the haze to catch us and take us back for some terrible, lengthy punishment. The sound of those big boots and the quickness of their approach were made worse by Finch's cackle from behind as he tried to keep control of the dogs.

"Mister Clawson," cried Madame Vickers. She was still twenty paces away, but her voice echoed through the darkness of early morning. Her arm raised up and a bony white finger pointed down the alley. "Those two belong to me. You would do well to give them back."

The hand on my neck clenched tighter, and the man knelt down beside us. There was a single lit streetlamp glowing dim over our heads and the sound of squeaking rats darting back and forth.

"I want you to go down these stairs," said Mister

Clawson. "And when you get to the bottom, I want you to open the door and go inside. Understood?"

"Understood." There was a surprising resolve in Thomas's voice, as though he knew instinctively that we should go down the stairs and open the door. I was not at all sure this was the best choice before us. Going back with Madame Vickers would be terrible, but going down *there*?

"*Mister* Clawson!" Madame Vickers was closing in on us. "I might remind you of your *obligations*."

It was clear the two of them knew each other and had established an arrangement neither Thomas nor I understood.

"Down the steps if you value your life!" yelled Mister Clawson, pushing the both of us and releasing us from his grip. He turned to the alley and crossed his massive arms over his chest, waiting for Madame Vickers to arrive. Thomas and I crept slowly into a swirling fog that hung thick and heavy over the stairs.

"Get on with it!" cried Mister Clawson. "You must go all the way into the mist, to the very bottom."

Faint light seeped around. Looking down, I saw the fog on the stairs had covered my legs. I stared at Thomas and he seemed like half a boy, the haze splitting him in two and leaving nothing below his shirtsleeves.

Into the mist. You must go all the way into the mist, to the very bottom.

Something about those words rang true, though I had no idea why. It was as though I'd heard them before, in a dream or a fractured memory.

Thomas and I continued down together, listening for the rats we could not see, wondering if we might step on a long, hairless tail and send one scratching and clawing up a pant leg.

"Where do you think you're going?" I lurched around and saw the long, crooked shadow of Madame Vickers standing at the very top of the stairs. "You shall come back right now or Finchy will let loose the dogs. You don't want to be down there all alone with the two of them in the dark!"

Where had Mister Clawson gone off to? He'd left us for dead! My whole body shook with fear and indecision. He'd trapped us for Madame Vickers and left us! I was thinking this awful thought and turned to Thomas in order to convince him that we should give up and go back to the House on the Hill, but when I opened my mouth to speak he screamed, and before my very eyes he disappeared into the mist.

"No!" shrieked Madame Vickers. "The dogs — send in the dogs!"

That was the last thing I remember hearing. *Send in the dogs!* The moment I heard those words someone — or something — grabbed me by the legs and pulled me so hard it took me right off my feet. I remember the sound of a slamming door, the clanging of metal, and the distant bark of Max and the Mooch.

And then there was nothing but a still, cold darkness and the sound of my own breathing.

CHAPTER 9

The Iron Door

"It took some nerve to come by way of Gaul's Ward."

It was the voice of Mister Clawson, accompanied by a thin line of orange light.

"Thomas?" I murmured into the gloom all around me.

"I'm here," came his voice, and then he touched me on the arm and we huddled close.

"It's good to have a brother at a time like this," bellowed Mister Clawson. His voice was unmistakable and close, as though his overgrown beard could scratch against us at any moment. I heard him scuffle toward the line of light at the floor.

"We thought you'd left us for dead," I mumbled into the shadows.

"I nearly did just that. If you'd listened from the start, it would have been quicker, easier. We wouldn't have had to deal with her. Now I'll have some explaining to do."

There came a grating sound as a heavy door was opened and the line of light on the floor grew wider until we could see the space around us and the room beyond the opening door. Where we were was perfectly square, and the only exit was the door that Mister Clawson had just opened and was passing through. When he was free of the room he pushed the door almost all the way shut with some effort. It was not closed all the way, leaving a long L of light seeping into the place where we sat. I touched the back of the wall we leaned on and found it was solid stone.

"How did we get in here?" asked Thomas. "There's no other door, only walls." He got up on his feet, tapping the three stone walls of the room. It was like the end of a short passageway with a tall ceiling. I could reach across and touch both sides. And there was simply no way out but the one door Mister Clawson had just opened. There ought to have been a door at our backs – where we had been sitting. That would have been where the bottom of the stairs led into the mist from which we'd come. But there was only a wall of impenetrable stone.

We turned together to face the door at the end of the passage. I was sure Mister Clawson could not be trusted. He could have kidnapped us for so many reasons, all of which seemed terrible as we stood in the small stone room.

"We couldn't turn back, even if we wanted to,"

said Thomas. "There's no going back to the House on the Hill. We're stuck in Gaul's Ward, and that door is our only way out." He pointed to the open door and began walking toward it.

"We never should have let ourselves get into this mess," I said.

Thomas seemed unshaken. "We're not dead yet. Maybe it won't be as bad as we think."

We went the rest of the way together and stood at the L of light near the door. It was closed too far to see past into the room beyond, so we put our shoulders into the door and pushed with all our might. It creaked and seemed to shred the earthen floor beneath it, but it opened far enough for us to sidestep through. I moved Thomas aside and went in first, holding my brother by the shirtsleeve as I went. Mister Clawson sat across from us at a large table lined all the way across the front with dripping, lit candles. He was not alone.

"Come closer, boys," said Mister Clawson. "She won't harm you. Unless, of course, I ask her to — in which case you'd be in a lot of trouble."

There was an animal sitting in front of the table — a very large animal unlike anything I'd ever seen. It looked an awful lot like a cat, only it was bigger than I was. I began to wonder how long and sharp its claws were.

"This is Thorn," said Mister Clawson. "I doubt you've ever seen a mountain lion before, but if you had, you'd know that Thorn is just such a creature. Under normal circumstances a mountain lion would tear the both of you apart."

Thorn stood up and walked toward us and my heart leaped into my throat. I should have cried out as she came near and purred into the air a few inches in front of my face, but I only managed a raspy whine as I tried aimlessly to reach for the door behind me with one hand.

"It's Thorn who gave me my name," Mister Clawson continued. Pulling up a sleeve that covered one of his hairy arms, he came over to us. There were deep scars that looked like claw marks all up and down his forearm. "Thorn gave me these the first time we met, but soon enough she and I worked things out to my liking."

"Are you her friend or her master?" asked Thomas.

The question amused Mister Clawson, and he laughed out loud. Thorn lifted a paw and began licking between her long, sharp claws.

"What do you think, Thorn? Am I your master?" Mister Clawson asked, rolling the sleeve back down and covering the scars on his arm.

Living all our lives either in the city of Ainsworth

or within the confines of the House on the Hill, Thomas and I had no practical knowledge of animals such as Thorn. We'd heard rumors of large creatures like bears and wolves, but the closest thing we'd ever seen were the stray cats that roamed the streets of Ainsworth and picked through the trash at Madame Vickers's. Maybe that was why — at the time — it didn't surprise either of us as much as one might suppose when Thorn purred deeply and we understood what her growling was meant to say. She did not speak as humans do; she spoke in her own language, with the slippery sounds of mountain lions and other big cats. It was this language we heard and understood.

"No human is my master."

She purred the words, dark and menacing in their tone, as though she were a being of few statements and this was one she'd run through her feline mind over and over again in the quiet of her thoughts. *No human is my master.*

"She belongs to me," said Mister Clawson, making it unclear whether he, too, understood what Thorn had said. "She does as I say, when I say."

"Thorn?" said my brother. Why was he so bold with a cat so big? He moved a hair closer to the mountain lion, and I almost leaped between them, afraid Thomas would get too close in his curiosity.

I feared a swift slash of a claw across his face, but Thorn remained still, waiting for Thomas to continue.

"Do you know the way to the Western Kingdom?"

When my brother put his mind to something, it was as though everything around him went blurry and only one thing stayed in focus until it was found or achieved. And so it was with his intent on reaching the Western Kingdom.

"I know the way," purred Thorn. The two stared forcefully at each other, and there seemed to be something unsaid passing between them.

Mister Clawson seemed perplexed. He began running the broad fingers of one hand through his coarse beard, watching the boy and the mountain lion. He seemed to guess that something was passing between the two, and it suddenly enraged him.

"Stop it! Stop it!" he finally yelled, but neither the big cat nor my brother seemed to notice. "I said stop it this instant!" He advanced on Thorn and was about to push Thomas aside when the mountain lion lashed in his direction, growling fiercely. Mister Clawson jumped back with a look of surprise on his face. He seemed for the first time to have lost command of the circumstances, though it lasted only a moment.

"How *dare* you show aggression toward *me*!"

Mister Clawson was in a rage, and Thorn was suddenly transformed into a creature who clearly felt the sting of her master's voice.

"Get under the table!" yelled Mister Clawson. Thorn moved off, the candlelight dancing slick on her gray coat, and she lay down in the shadows.

"Both of you, up on your feet! Come with me," shouted Mister Clawson. His voice had a sharpness to it, every word a knife. He went past the table, taking a candle in his hand as he went, and led us down a darkened path with a high stone archway for a ceiling. Mold covered the walls and cold, clammy water dripped on our heads. The farther we went, the more the passageway was alive with crawling bugs and the thick smell of deep earth. Mister Clawson had to duck lower and lower as we went until he crouched so near to the ground his eyes were level with ours. After a time he stopped, turning to us with the yellow candlelight glowing before his face. A drop of water landed on his nose, and he wiped it down into his beard. Everything about his face glistened, and he appeared to me as something of a madman, crouched in the corner like a wild animal about to pounce on us.

"There is a way known only to a few," he began. His voice had gone from a raging torrent to a low, rumbling presence, as though he were sharing sacred information. "A way that begins when you go into the mist and continues here." Mister Clawson moved to one side and held out the candle. There was only a little light, but it was enough to reveal a small iron door with a thick handle in the very middle. Beneath the handle, etched deep into the iron, was the symbol of square and circle — the very one from Mingleton's saddlebag and our knees.

I glanced at Thomas and he glanced at me, both our eyes bulging with surprise. I had no memory of this place, and yet how could it be that the sign on this hidden door beneath Gaul's Ward could also appear on our knees?

Mister Clawson looked at the two of us again, covering the door with his body.

"It is here that you will go — with Thorn accompanying you. You must come back with the thing I tell you to bring. Do you understand?"

I didn't understand at all, but it was an oddly invigorating idea to venture through a door that might hold the answers to questions I'd asked all my life.

Mister Clawson's face grew dark and threatening. "There is no other way out of Gaul's Ward for you now. This is your dark path to walk, and you *will* bring me what I require."

It was clear to us then that if we did not succeed

at whatever Mister Clawson had planned, he would do away with us.

As if to drive the point home, a drop of water hit the candle. The flame fizzled out, and in the darkness Mister Clawson told us where we were to go and what we were to bring back.

Behind the Iron Door

"Thorn will guide the way. She knows the way out and the way back in." The voice of Mister Clawson was almost a whisper, as if he were speaking of things he wanted to keep a secret even as he let them drift out of his mouth. "It won't take you more than two days to make the trip." He pulled a satchel out from behind him in the darkness and held it out to me. "You keep the food and the water."

I took the satchel out of his hand, trying to guess what was inside by its weight and shape. It wasn't very heavy, so I knew right away there wouldn't be very much water inside.

"Now listen!" said Mister Clawson. "Thorn will take you to the place, just as I told you. You need only bring back as much as that bag will hold. Eat the food on the way there, or put it in your pockets if you have to. Just fill the bag as much as you can before you return."

"What are we filling it with?" asked Thomas with an air of distrust.

"Whatever Thorn tells you to fill it with, *just as*

I told you before! Now go on! The sun will be up soon, and it will be hot where you're going."

"But won't we be seen by someone in Ainsworth?" asked Thomas. "They'll send us back to Madame Vickers's House on the Hill."

Mister Clawson's loathsome cackle filled the air. "Where you're going, no person will see. That's one thing you can be sure of."

Thorn snarled, and this time went through the iron door. I didn't understand the sounds she made as I had before. I began to wonder if I'd only imagined understanding them. Maybe we were under some sort of spell cast by Mister Clawson. Maybe he had made it seem as though Thorn were speaking to us in order to trick us.

"Go!" cried Mister Clawson. "You don't want to keep that cat waiting any longer than you have to." He lit a new candle and held out the single flame for one of us to take. Thomas took it clumsily, yelping as wax dripped down on his hand.

"Get on with it!" bellowed Mister Clawson, pushing the both of us toward Thorn and the doorway before retreating and blocking our other possible exit. We were trapped between a very large, frightening mountain lion and an even larger, angry man. Things were not going as well as we'd hoped they might upon leaving the care of Madame Vickers.

"That's a nice kitty." I began, followed a moment later by Thomas in his most soothing voice, "Here, kitty, kitty, kitty. . . ."

The light from the candle didn't reach very far — only enough to see a little of what was before us.

"Quickly now," Thorn growled. "We have a long way to go, and not much time to get there."

Thomas held the light out as far as he could, and we both saw the gleaming cat's eyes attached to the head from which the voice had come.

"How far is it?" asked Thomas, as if the idea of a mountain lion we could understand was a small detail we could ignore altogether. Thorn didn't answer, but turned away instead and faced toward the iron door. Thomas and I whispered quietly to each other.

"Did you hear what she said?"

"Yes, I think I did."

"Maybe we can trust her. She doesn't seem to want to eat us."

"I wish we had something to defend ourselves with."

"I wish we could get something to eat out of that bag."

"I wish Mister Clawson were a chicken. Thorn would probably eat a chicken."

This was something we had done whenever we found ourselves unbearably bored picking through the trash on the hill. Back and forth we would go, telling what we wished, usually trying to make the other laugh. It was a good way to pass the time or keep one's mind off of the idea that we'd stumbled into so much trouble so quickly.

"I wish Finch and Thorn were locked in a room together. I think Finch would pee his pants."

"I wish Mister Clawson was a baker, and he baked us a big fat cake, and he put it in the bag with a giant jug of milk."

"I wish the two of you would stop talking so much and open the iron door so we can be on our way!" Thorn's growl filled the small space. She sat in front of the door, off to one side, her silvery fur shining like glass in the soft light.

"You do it," said Thomas. "I've got the candle to hold."

I reached a shaking hand past Thorn's face toward the latch, wondering if my arm was about to be clawed to pieces. But Thorn just sniffed the air, looking curiously at my trembling hand upon the handle.

"I wish there was a pile of candy behind this door, and a nice bed to sleep on, and a warm bath to wash up in," I said.

I turned the handle and it made a sound of old stone on old metal.

"One of your wishes is about to come true," said

89

Thorn. *Really?* I thought. Could there really be a soft bed or a stash of candy or a warm bath waiting on the other side? I pulled on the iron door and it slowly opened with a dark howl. I half expected a torrent of bats to escape into the passageway, but instead I felt only the glow of warm air.

"Don't look down," growled Thorn.

A moment later she was gone, through the door and down into the soft yellow glow of the world beyond the iron door. Thomas and I waited, looking through the small opening the door had covered, terrified at what we might find as we neared the opening. Thomas blew out the candle, but soft yellow light remained, glowing like a vast liquid sky from somewhere beyond the iron door.

"Hurry back!" came an echoing voice from the other end of the passage. It was Mister Clawson, far away now, his voice small but mean. "And close that door behind you!"

I crept up to the very edge of the door and looked down. Thorn had told me not to do it, and the moment I did, I wished I'd heeded her warning. There was a ladder leading down much farther than I'd imagined it was possible to go into the belly of the world. At the very bottom was a faint, glowing sea of water that seemed to go on forever.

Thorn was perched on a small platform of rocks jutting out from the stone face that held the ladder.

"You don't want to fall, so hold the ladder tightly as you go."

With frightening quickness, Thorn jumped across the ladder, landing on another formation of rocks and skidding to a stop. The formations were scattered all the way down the side of the wall, crisscrossing the ladder as they went.

I turned toward Thomas and put my legs out into the opening of the door, stepping down onto the first few rungs.

"Don't look down, don't look down, don't look down," I repeated to myself. I looked up and saw Thomas's head poking out over the edge. "Try not to kick dirt in my face."

"I wish Mister Clawson was a chicken," he repeated, looking back once more in the direction of our captor.

Before long we were in something of a pattern, Thomas and I making wishes as we went, while Thorn bounded back and forth beneath us on our way to the very bottom. The air was warm and humid, like a hot summer day after a morning of rain, and soon I was thinking about how much work it would be to go back up the ladder. I don't know how much time passed, but there came a moment when I no longer heard Thorn bounding from one perch to another and I glanced down for the first time since our journey began. She was standing at the bottom, at the edge of the water, looking up at us.

"We're almost there, Thomas!" I said. "Only a few more steps to go and we've done it."

When there were three rungs left to go I jumped down and landed on flat, cracked rock that looked old and wrinkly. A moment later Thomas found his way to the bottom as well, and we stood next to Thorn looking out over the watery world.

"What is this place?" asked Thomas, his voice trailing off as he gazed out into the open.

"It's the Lake of Fire," purred Thorn. There was dread in the sound of her voice.

"I was hoping for the pile of candy," I muttered, "not the warm bath."

Thorn began walking along the edge of the soft glowing water. It looked as though the edge dropped off very deep, and I was careful to keep a few feet away from it as we followed Thorn.

"Is it hot?" Thomas asked. "Will it burn my hand if I touch it?"

"Don't touch it!" I said to Thomas. "Who knows what it will do to you. For all we know it might shrivel your hand into a prune."

"The water won't hurt you," said Thorn. "What's *in* the water is what we need to be careful of."

We walked on — scared half to death at the thought of something slithering out of the water at our feet and dragging us in. We went along the edge about twenty steps, and then I couldn't go any farther.

"We can't just keep blindly following you," I said. Thorn glanced back at us and saw that we'd stopped. I was afraid of Thorn, but more afraid of where she might be leading us. "For all we know we could be walking to our deaths. Maybe we're a sacrifice or something horrible like that. And why can we understand what you're saying? You're an *animal*! We shouldn't be able to understand what you're saying."

Thorn had that look a cat has when they're sizing up their prey. A deep, eye-piercing look that made me wonder if she was about to pounce on us both and drop us over the edge into the Lake of Fire.

"We only need to walk a little more," she purred. "There's a boat that will take us where we need to go. I'll answer your questions while we glide across the Lake of Fire."

Thorn walked on without us while Thomas and I whispered to each other. The idea of getting any closer than we already were to the water — let alone getting *on* the water — was not appealing.

"We could go back up the ladder," I whispered. "Maybe Mister Clawson has gone, and we could sneak away."

"The water doesn't look that hot," Thomas replied. To my horror he scampered over to the edge and put his hand in, touching his finger to his lips to see what it tasted like. While his hand hadn't been boiled a bright red, he did make a sour face at the taste in his mouth. I joined him at the waters edge and knelt down.

"What's it taste like?" I asked.

"Like a bowl of salt," said Thomas. "I don't think it's drinkable."

There came a strange sound from somewhere far off on the water, like something moving and growing in velocity as it moved. Far off, where we couldn't see, it sounded as though air had boiled over into quaking bubbles onto the surface of the lake.

"Let's go back," I said, pulling Thomas by the shirtsleeve and backing away from the water. "Let's just get out of here and do whatever Mister Clawson makes us do."

Thomas stared at me, and I knew what he was thinking before he said it.

"I'm following Thorn," he told me. "She hasn't hurt us yet, and I think she wants to help us. She's not going out on the water unless it's safe, right? So as long as we stick together, we're all right."

"What if she pushes us off?" I asked.

The idea of floundering in the Lake of Fire

seemed to fall on deaf ears. Once Thomas had made up his mind to go adventuring, there was no turning him around. Even at the risk of both our lives, there was no way to stop him. I had no choice but to follow behind as he started off in the direction Thorn had gone.

It was a short walk along flat, cracked stones. The light was faint but pleasant, and it went slowly dimmer and then bright again, like a very slow heartbeat. The face of the water was as still as glass. It looked like I could walk out as far as I wanted, watching my reflection as I went. It was mesmerizing, the way it was so still, like a mirror.

"This will take some work," Thorn said as we came up beside her. There was a perfectly square object on the water, and Thorn jumped onto it. The whole thing was about the size of two wooden horse carts laid side by side, and there was nothing on it. It looked as though it was black, but I couldn't tell for sure. When Thorn jumped on, it bobbed erratically, rippling the glassy surface of the water. Thomas wasted no time leaping onto the strange floating object next, and I followed. Feeling its unsteady wobble beneath me made my empty stomach roll.

"Welcome to the Lake of Fire," said Thorn. "Best to speak in whispers, for there are some we don't want to meet along the way."

As if on cue, the strange sound of great bubbles breaking on the surface of the water returned from far off in the distance. We were on the Lake of Fire, and the vessel we were on was pointed in the precise direction of the monstrous noise.

"What's that sound?" I whispered, but I got no reply as the makeshift boat we were on sat peacefully along the edge of a vast body of glowing yellow water.

CHAPTER 11

A Clanging Chain
on the Lake of Fire

The way in which the square black vessel — I'll call it our raft — was to make its way across the Lake of Fire was not how one might expect. There were no oars or sails, nothing that we could use to propel the raft from one side of the lake to the other.

"How do we make it move?" I asked. The raft bobbed up and down gently, but it wasn't going anywhere.

"There," purred Thorn, raising her paw toward the sky before us. The light that was all around us came from beneath the lake, and it quickly faded until there was only darkness a few feet over our heads. It was the strangest thing to see such soft light in so vast a space, a light that turned to darkness more quickly than it should have. I hadn't seen what Thorn was showing us until she pointed it out. There were chains dangling down from overhead, and at the very end of the chains were hooks. The first of these chains hung down ten feet away from us over the Lake of Fire, far enough out that we couldn't reach it. The one after that was another ten feet, and on it went like that, a line of perfectly still chains hanging from a stone ceiling somewhere far above where we could not see. The chains seemed to hang from a black sky as if by magic, and they had an awful, silent stillness about them that made a person want to push and clang them together.

"We must push away from the edge to reach the first chain," said Thorn. "But we must be careful not to miss. If we drift off the line of chains — *anywhere* along the line of chains — we will be lost on the Lake of Fire."

"This gets better all the time, don't you think?" I groused to Thomas, but he seemed entranced by the idea of pulling himself along the line of chains and didn't respond.

"The two of you sit in the middle. I've done this before," Thorn continued. "Don't touch the chain when we come beneath it. There are dangers on the Lake of Fire that can be awakened. Let me show you before you touch them."

I took a last look at the ledge and the way back to the ladder, thinking for a moment I might bolt for the way out and take my chances with Mister Clawson. But Thomas was already seated in the middle of the raft, perfectly content to ride out into the unknown. I crawled over to the center of the raft and sat down beside him.

Thorn jumped off the raft, back onto land, and I was suddenly aware that we might have been tricked, that she might push us out into the Lake of Fire and leave us as dinner for some unseen monster beneath the surface. My worry increased as I watched Thorn push us out with her two front legs, springing hard back to land as she did so. She stood on the flat stones we'd left behind and watched as we drifted out toward the first still chain.

I stood up in a panic, afraid of what would happen to us — but I needn't have worried so much. As I was trying to stand, Thorn leaped from the bank and flew toward the raft. The force of her landing sent the raft bobbing on the water toward the first of the chains.

"We'll need that extra little bit to catch hold of the first one," Thorn growled. There was a resolve in her voice I hadn't heard before as she centered her attention on the chain.

"Move to the side now," she said. "Leave me the middle of the raft."

Thomas and I began to move to the same side, causing the raft to lean hard toward the glowing yellow water. Thorn scowled but didn't take her eyes from the chain. Thomas wasted no time scurrying back across the middle to the other side, where he bent down on his knees and waited.

The raft slowed on our approach to the first chain. It felt as though the yellow water was thick like honey and would not let us go.

"Come on," purred Thorn quietly. "Don't stop now."

The raft wasn't moving any longer. We had come to a halt with the chain too far away to reach. Thorn growled in a way that I could not understand, backed up two or three paces, and ran for the edge of the raft. When she reached the very edge she jumped and soared into the air, catching the chain with her sharp claws. She swung violently away from us, disappearing into the dark, then started back, her full weight and size coming furiously toward us.

"Grab hold!" she growled. As she came over the raft she dropped out of the air — and, quick as a whip, Thomas was up off his knees. Thorn crashed into the raft and spun uncontrolled, digging her claws into wood as her back legs dangled precariously over the edge. The chain flew high into the air. When it came slashing down out of the darkness, Thomas reached both hands up and caught it by the hook, holding steady at the center of the raft.

"Now pull on it as hard as you can," said Thorn. "And don't let it go until I tell you to."

Thomas heaved on the chain and the raft began moving slowly forward.

"Pull as hard as you can!" commanded Thorn.

Thomas kept pulling and we gained speed, though only a little, and it looked to me like we were heading in just the right direction. When we came to a place where the chain was hanging straight down again and it would do no good to keep pulling on it, Thorn told Thomas to gently let it go, which he did.

"It will be easier now," said Thorn, a sense of relief in her feline voice. And so it was. For the chains were closer together as we went, and we needed only to be sure and go in the right direction, gently pulling on each of the chains as they came near, making our way across the Lake of Fire.

Thomas and I settled into a routine of taking turns at the chains, and we began to ask questions that Thorn was surprisingly willing to answer. The farther we ventured away from Mister Clawson, the more comfortable she became and the less frightened of her I felt. It was a journey across soft, glowing water in which we learned a great deal about her circumstances, what had brought her to Mister Clawson, and the extraordinary journey we found ourselves on.

You, Alexa, know what it's like to be close to

animals and have them trust you with their stories. But you must understand how different it was back then. When Thomas and I were in our youth, it wasn't just us that seemed young. Everything in The Land of Elyon was younger. If you can imagine, people and wild animals did not come into contact. We stayed in our place and they stayed in theirs. Of course we had domesticated animals — horses, dogs, cats, livestock — but we stayed entirely away from places that held mysterious creatures of the untamed variety. Wolves, great bears, mountain lions — even squirrels.

Some animals were more inclined to mix with humans, while others were set against the idea from the start and fought to maintain separation. Certain places began to feel almost haunted. There were places you simply didn't go, places where a human felt entirely unwelcome, where it felt as though you were being watched by menacing forces. The Great Ravine, the Dark Hills, the Sly Field, Fenwick Forest, the mountains — these places were for wild animals, not for people. There was something magical, both dark and light, that kept the two worlds apart.

As we traveled, Thorn took great care to explain to us the reasons why man and beast stayed away from one another in vast areas of The Land of Elyon. Both understood that bringing the two together was a dangerous path in which the oldest magic could be put at risk. Animals such as wolves and bears called humans "magic killers," while humans felt a great fear of places they didn't know or understand. It was this fear that drove humans to hate wild animals and places, and begin to wonder how to bring these things under their control.

This had created something of a silent war between the two. If men came into the wild, animals didn't so much try to kill them as scare them, to warn them to stay away.

Humans *are* the killers of magic, you see. We must accept this unfortunate fact of life. Think about it, though I know you don't want to. People can be cruel, unkind, mean, selfish. We can be a great many dreadful things, and at one time or another we are all guilty of bad behavior. What we fail to realize is that we are the *only* ones who can do such things. All the animals — *all of them* — are innocent. The trees, the flowers, the streams and mountains — all are innocent. But we do not enjoy such innocence. We are the killers of magic, whether we like it or not.

And so we have a choice. We can fight against our dark nature or we can give in to it. Back then, if you happened upon the right place, you could understand a wild animal. It was as if a bridge appeared — a kind of intercession, if you will — in

which their way of speaking and ours were connected. And so you must imagine a man such as
Mister Clawson finding one of these places and
bringing a wild animal into his midst – *understanding* that animal, if only for a brief time – and
then finding a way of keeping the animal under his
control. If you can imagine these things, then you
are very near to understanding Thorn.

"Children are different," Thorn told us as
Thomas pulled on a chain and let it go so that it
hung perfectly still behind us as we drifted past.
"They don't bring harm in the same way adults do.
I don't know why, but a child wandering in the forest kills no magic and does no damage. But that
doesn't mean a pack of wolves wouldn't want to
tear you to bits. The untamed regions are just
that – *untamed* – and dinner is dinner."

I didn't want to think about being devoured by
wild animals, so I tried to think of something different to ask Thorn. The next chain was coming
near and it was mine to take hold of. Grabbing it,
I asked: "How did you come to be with Mister
Clawson?"

Thorn appeared to gaze back into a past she had
trouble remembering.

"My family used to come from the mountain to
the Great Ravine and hunt during a certain time
of the year. There was a cave near our hunting

ground that my mother told me to stay away from. She caught me near there once and punished me severely. It made me angry – the way she got so upset and wouldn't trust me – so I went back the next day when she was hunting and I ventured inside the cave."

There was a moment of silence when I thought she wouldn't go on, but it passed. "Mister Clawson was in the cave, hiding in the dark. It was my first time in the hunting grounds at the Great Ravine and I wasn't very big then. I clawed and clawed at him, trying to get away, but I failed."

"And now he keeps you in that room with the candles?" asked Thomas sadly.

"Sometimes he sends me back through the mouth of the cave to get something for him, but yes, mostly I stay in the room with the candles."

"Why don't you escape? Why not just leave and never come back?"

Evidently these were hard questions for Thorn to answer, for she turned her head to the side and wouldn't look at us.

"The two of you won't survive in the wild without me to protect you. He only sends me out with children such as you, because he knows I won't let you perish. Without me you might already be dead. And when we reach the wild, there is no hope for you but to stay with me."

It was suddenly clear to me that Thorn was the closest thing to a friend Thomas and I could have dreamed of. A two-hundred-pound beast with claws as long as my toes was our guide and our shield! And she'd been lost as a cub herself. She knew the sorrow of being young and alone. She would never let that happen to me or Thomas.

"Thank you, Thorn," I said, releasing the chain and stepping out of the way for Thomas to take his turn. "We've needed a friend for a long time." I knelt down before the great cat and all my fear of her was gone. There was a sonlike feeling in its place, as though she were our mother and we were her cubs, and nothing in the world would let her fail in defending us against the wild world outside.

"How did Mister Clawson come to be in the cave?" asked Thomas.

"He found the iron door — a door no animal can open on its own — and he followed the same path we now travel. He's someone who lives in the realms of dark magic, and when you live there, certain forces are apt to find you and drag you away."

"What do you mean?" asked Thomas, pulling on the chain and releasing it softly.

"I mean Mister Clawson dabbled in dark magic in dark places, and eventually that choice led here, to the Lake of Fire. It's here that Abaddon lives, deep beneath the world."

The sound of that name — *Abaddon* — had a curious feel to it. I whispered it to myself — *Abaddon* — and it felt as though I were calling some dark spirit of power closer to us. The name tingled on my lips and I wished I hadn't spoken it.

"There is good magic — the kind of Elyon — and evil magic — the kind of Abaddon," continued Thorn. "There can't be one without the other. The room you were pulled into, the iron door, the Lake of Fire — these are all within the realm of dark magic, and together they are a secret passage to the untamed places of the world."

"Pulled into?" I asked.

Thorn explained that it was Mister Clawson who had pulled us into the room with only one door. His arm came through the stones and took hold of us, and we went right through to the other side.

Mister Clawson had very limited powers, but this one he had mastered — to bring those he chose into his realm and put them to work on tasks of his choosing.

Thorn, I was finding, had not learned certain motherly traits in the charge of Mister Clawson. She did not wonder if something might scare us or bother us. She simply answered the questions put to her.

"The iron door is a passageway down into the

world of darkness and out into the wild. If a man can get hold of a wild beast — *control* one — within this world of darkness, he can gain for himself a way to 'cross between the two worlds unharmed. *If...*" She paused. "If he can find those that would do his traveling for him."

"That's where we come in," Thomas suggested. Then, thinking a little more, he added, "What exactly are we getting for Mister Clawson?"

Thorn didn't answer. Changing her tone she stared past us into the glowing water.

"We come to the end of the chains."

It was dimmer on this side — it had been getting dimmer as we went without us really noticing — so that both Thomas and I were surprised to find the raft bumping softly against rock, wobbling back and forth on impact. I had a hold on the last chain, and when we hit the rocks, I jerked forward just enough to flip the chain up out of my hands into the air. It folded over itself, the links running back down like dripping water, clanging softly as they came.

All was still as I steadied the chain in my hand and let it go, thinking nothing of the tiny ringing noise I'd let slip over the Lake of Fire. Thorn's ears were perked and listening. She looked at us as if to say, *Don't make a sound.* But it was too late, for somewhere in the distance, high over our heads and down the length of the Lake of Fire, the noise of a thousand screaming voices came bellowing over the water.

"Run for the wall!" Thorn roared. "The bats have awakened!"

CHAPTER 12

The Great Ravine

Thorn jumped from the raft first and beckoned us to follow. She was much faster than we were, and we quickly fell behind. The leathery sound of beating wings filled the air behind us, and the shrieking of the bats made me cover my ears as we ran. It was an awful, piercing sound that grew more frightening by the second.

Thorn was already to the wall, running back and forth in the faint light, searching for something.

"Here! Here it is!" she cried. "Hurry!"

Breathless and confused, we came alongside Thorn and saw she was standing before a second iron door. It was just the same as the one above that led to Mister Clawson's chamber with the candles, and it had the same square and circle symbol beneath the handle. Were we somehow tied to this dark passage? Who had put the markings on our skin and where were we being led?

"Turn the handle and open the door," Thorn instructed. She was calm in the face of great danger, but her eyes told me we'd better hurry if we were going to escape the Lake of Fire. Thomas was down on his knees in a flash, trying with all his might to turn the handle. I joined him, putting my hands tightly next to his, and we both tried to force the handle down. It budged slightly, then all at once gave way, the sound of iron on iron clashing through the air. This seemed to send the bats into an even greater fury, and, looking back, I could see a black cloud moving fast and low over the glowing water. Beneath the moving black cloud the Lake of Fire boiled up orange and bright.

"Open the door!" cried Thorn, her claws biting into the stone wall where iron met rock.

Thomas and I heaved on the handle of the iron door, and it creaked open with a maddening slowness. The moment a small crack appeared, Thorn attacked it with her claws, pulling the door toward us. It was scary to be so close to such a big animal doing such powerful work. She snarled violently, pitting all of her will against the iron door.

"Through the door, both of you! As fast as you can!"

Thomas fought his way through the thin opening first. The opening was barely big enough for us to shimmy through, and when it was my turn and I popped through on the other side, my pack was caught, pinning me to the door. Thomas pulled on my hands and Thorn pushed once with her claws from behind – knocking the bag free – and I tumbled forward onto cold earth.

The opening wasn't big enough for Thorn, and looking back I saw that Thomas was pushing against the door, trying to get it open far enough for her to fit inside. The bats were very close, but the more frightening sound was that of whatever was making its way to the surface of the Lake of Fire. It was a horrible, deep sound that made me want to run in the opposite direction. It took all my courage to join Thomas at the iron door and push, opening our hidden space to bats and monsters I could not see.

Thorn clawed mercilessly at the opening as we forced the door open far enough for her to slip through. With a final thrust of her powerful legs she broke free and tumbled in at our feet.

"They're coming! We have to close the door!" screamed Thomas. It was hard to make out his words over the roar of bats. The front assault of the black wave of flapping leather wings had reached the door, and no amount of effort would get the door closed before some of them got through. There was a straight bar of metal on this side of the iron door, long enough for two people to grab hold and pull. I held the bar on top and Thomas held it on the bottom, both of us pulling hard and fast.

Bats began to flow through the crack in the door like thick black leaves blown free in a violent thunderstorm. As they came through, Thorn batted them to the ground with vicious slashes. One after the other she broke their bodies until we had the door closed far enough that no more could fit through. The few bats that were missed by Thorn alighted on the ceiling, unexpectedly lost from the black cloud of the swarm and unsure what to do.

"Get it all the way closed!" growled Thorn, batting the air with her claws in search of renegade bats flying low in the cave. "It will come out of the water for a dreadful moment if it sees the door is open to the wild."

The bats were so loud crashing and slashing outside the door, all other sounds from the Lake of Fire had been drowned out. But suddenly there was a new noise, and the bats moved off as fast as they'd come. Something else — something entirely more savage and evil — was coming for the door. It sounded slippery and heavy, a dread beast coming from the Lake of Fire, sniffing the air and smelling two boys from Madame Vickers's House on the Hill.

Seeing the terror in Thomas's face and hearing the sound of the approaching beast sent my mind reeling, and all at once I knew what to do.

"Get away from the door!" I ordered Thomas. I forced him back, took the handle firmly in both hands, and braced my feet on the wall to the right of the iron door. It was difficult holding such an awkward position, but I was able to force the door toward me those last few inches before feeling my hands slip free and falling back hard onto the ground of the cave. Looking up I saw Thorn slash at the handle I'd held, turning it bit by bit until she'd locked the iron door once more.

There were two or three bats circling drunkenly in the air above us, bouncing against the door as if they'd lost their way. The dirt floor of the cave was littered with dead bats, their murky blood oozing at our feet.

"We're safe for now," said Thorn. Winded, she flopped down on the floor with Thomas and me, licking the blood on her paws. It was difficult to tell if she was licking at her own wounded claws or the spilled blood of the bats she'd destroyed.

"What was that *thing*?" asked Thomas. "It sounded like nothing I've ever heard before."

Thorn stood, staring toward the unseen ceiling of rocks somewhere above. Her head lolled slowly from side to side, like one of the cats at the House on the Hill waiting to strike a fly out of the air. Then she leaped straight up, slashing hard, and one of the few remaining bats crashed against the wall. Thorn turned and looked at Thomas.

"I've never seen what's in the Lake of Fire, so I can only guess at how big it is, how many teeth it has, how black and slick its monstrous head must be. I'm just happy that door is closed and we're all on this side of it." Thorn gazed back and forth between the two of us. "You could have left me behind, but you stayed. I won't forget that."

Until then, my attention had been on Thorn, the awful sounds coming from behind the iron door, and the immense struggle to free ourselves from the Lake of Fire. But now my mind caught up to my senses, and it came as a surprise that there was still light in the cave, though the iron door was shut. From where did the light come?

"Follow me," whispered Thorn. "Stay close and silent as we make our way. You must watch my steps and do the same. Don't veer off the path or fall behind."

Thorn moved away from the iron door and quickly disappeared down a narrow path. Thomas and I quickly stood and followed. The path turned steep and treacherous, but we were delighted to find that the faint light of the cave grew stronger as we went. It was a strange sensation of going down deeper into the earth at a very steep grade and yet finding the light around us growing in intensity as we kept on. The path was cut with sharp stones that made good footings, and there were sudden twists and turns where we could take hold of the narrow walls surrounding us.

This went on for some time without a word between us, until the floor leveled off and Thorn glanced back at us.

"We come now to the last turn," she said. "The world of men is behind you now. Only the wild remains."

She went on, around the last tight turn where we couldn't see her, and I said to Thomas, "Who'd have thought it would come to this so swiftly?"

I expected to find Thomas in a state of fear, unwilling to go around the last turn — but I should have known better. Thomas could not have hoped for a better outcome than the one we'd stumbled into. We'd only been free a day, and already we'd found our way into more adventure than I thought could be found in a lifetime of searching.

"Let's round the corner together," said Thomas. His sharp green eyes flashed with excitement, and the two of us took the last few steps out of the cave.

We'd spent a night running from Finch and the dogs, only to be captured by Mister Clawson and pulled into his world of dark magic. It had been a long and shadowy journey with very little light along the way. When we stepped out into the path of the blinding sun, it made us cover our eyes. If you've ever woken from a nap in the middle of the day with the sun over your head, then you know the feeling — the feeling when darkness turns to light all at once.

"Stay right where you are," said Thorn. "And don't make a sound."

I struggled to open my eyes, looking first at the jagged rocks and dust beneath my feet, then slowly lifting my gaze upward. There were rocks of deep red and brown shooting up across a vast and dangerous-looking valley below. We were perched well above the ground, and yet we were much closer to the bottom of the walls of jagged rocks than we were to the tops. It felt like we'd come out of a pin-hole in an enormous wall of stone that rose above and beneath us. To the left, a lifeless valley widened and grew shallower, until somewhere off in the distance it leveled off with cliffs before the sea. To the right it grew narrower and deeper, until I could only wonder at what might live in such a place.

"I gather we're not going that way," said Thomas, pointing toward the wide, rising end of the valley. "That would be the way back to Ainsworth, if I have my bearings right."

Thorn nodded her great head and whispered back, "We must go deeper into the wild to find what Mister Clawson seeks. I know the way. But first we'll rest a while, so you can eat and drink what's in your pack."

She walked back into the cave, and when she did, I saw that she'd been hiding something from us. She'd been standing before a stunningly narrow and steep path with a wall on one side and open air on the other.

We were in the Great Ravine, the sun casting spiked shadows on the stone walls that surrounded us, a treacherous path along which to make our way.

We had come into a place where no man or woman was welcome – a place of deep magic both light and dark – at a time when there were no walls or towns to speak of between us and the Western Kingdom.

PART 2

Into the Wild

In the forest wanders the bear, fierce
and menacing, and yet innocent.
—Fyodor Dostoyevsky,
The Brothers Karamazov, 1880

❧ CHAPTER 13 ❧
A MAGICAL NIGHT

It had been a breathless day of listening to Roland tell his tale. The sun was hanging heavy on the water as he came to the place in his story in which he, Thomas, and Thorn returned to the cave and ate what little food they had. I stood and stretched my back, wondering whether or not we'd come to the end of what Roland would tell us that day. There was a glimmer in his eye that told me we might have a night of legend yet to come, a night in which Yipes and I would hear about the Great Ravine, Fenwick Forest, Mount Norwood — all of them *before* the time of the walls. What a strange thought it was to imagine all these places without Bridewell tucked in between them, without my home of Lathbury, without the other towns of Lunenburg and Turlock. I was dying to hear what it was like before Thomas Warvold ventured into the wild and built the walls and the towns of Bridewell Common.

"I'll make up a pot of soup!" cried Yipes. "That's just what we need to keep things adrift. It will be the finest soup the crew of this vessel has ever enjoyed, and I'll bring bread and hot tea. We can stay all night at the wheel if we like, can't we? Tomorrow is just another day with the wide and Lonely Sea before us. We can sleep late if we want to!"

121

It was possible Yipes wanted to hear the rest of the story even more than I did. To imagine Mount Norwood before he'd been there and built his little house on the stream was something I was sure he could hardly wait to hear more about.

"And *you!*" He pointed at me with his tiny index finger. "You will help me. I'm not taking any chances that there might be talk of something important while I'm busy over there." He pointed off toward the cabin, then back at me. "You must come with me, give him a bit of rest. He needs a chance to catch his breath before he gets on with the tale."

"Bring the soup," said Roland. "We'll have to see how well you cook tonight before I decide what to do with my evening." He yawned loudly, raising his hands up off the wheel and over his head. "I am feeling a tad sleepy, to tell the truth."

Yipes was shaking all over, his eyes darting back and forth and his fingers fumbling in search of something to do. He was in a high state of alarm.

"The tea will be just the thing!" he cried. "We have some of the black tea — not that awful sleepy kind — and I'm sure it will perk you right up!" Yipes grabbed me by the hand and began to haul me across the deck. "Not to worry!" he carried on as we made our way to the cabin.

An hour later, the sun and wind were both gone and an unnatural calm enveloped the deck of the *Warwick Beacon*. It was rare for the ship to sit so very still and quiet with the sails still up. Yipes was bringing the kettle of soup and would be a moment. I had already brought the bowls, cups, and bread and had set them on an old brown blanket that I'd thrown over the deck at the base of the wheel. I had the pot of tea with me, and I put it on the blanket. I was about to go back for the blankets from our hammocks to warm us as the night grew colder.

"We have stopped," whispered Roland. He let go of the wheel. "I wonder what force has brought us to this place to wait?"

"What do you mean?" I questioned.

"There's always wind on the Lonely Sea. Even if it's very little, there's always something. The sails are empty and the water is still like a mountain lake at dusk. We're not going anywhere until the Lonely Sea lets us proceed."

Roland let go of the wheel and it did not stir. He took the wooden pin in his hand and locked the wheel in place for good measure, then walked to the very front of the boat and looked at the rising moon.

"It will be a nice full moon tonight," he said. "That light will keep us good company, don't you think?"

He didn't look toward me, but I nodded anyway and raced back to the cabin to get more blankets. As I bounded down the steps I didn't see Yipes coming up, and the two of us collided. Poor Yipes held the kettle of soup by the handles on each side and staggered backward down the three steps he had come up, the kettle swinging wildly in his hands. He managed to keep hold of the main part of our dinner and bring the kettle under control at the bottom of the stairs, but he was a nervous wreck as he stood sighing with relief.

"Here, you take it up. I'm afraid I'll drop it," said Yipes, holding the steaming kettle of soup out to me.

"You get the blankets," I said. "It might get chilly out tonight if he goes on for very long. I don't want there to be any excuses for him to let up." I took the kettle from Yipes's shaking, outstretched hands. "And bring the lid for this pot. We don't want it to get cold too quickly."

I carefully made my way up the stairs with the soup. Soon Yipes had retrieved the blankets and the lid for the kettle and was anxiously nudging me along on the deck. He reached up and placed the lid on the kettle with a clang, and a moment later we arrived at the place where our dinner picnic was to occur. It was a magical setting I won't soon forget: steaming soup and tea on the deck of a weather-beaten ship with a thousand tales of its own to tell, the moon casting a pale light on the steam rising from our bowls and cups. The smells of spices and tea hung in the still air, no wind to blow them off, and even Roland couldn't help feeling the thrill of the moment.

"Well, it does seem like a night for a story," he said, taking a spoonful of soup and slurping it down. "And the soup is better than usual, I must admit."

"And the tea. What about the tea?" asked Yipes, his thick brown eyebrows and mustache all raised in anticipation of Roland's answer.

"I believe it has revived me. I feel I could stay up a while longer."

Yipes was so pleased to have kept the captain awake and happy that he laughed out loud and gave me a shove on the shoulder that made the teacup in my hand wobble, spilling a drop or two of its contents onto the blanket over my legs.

"I enjoyed a brief moment of peace with Thomas and Thorn on that morning, not so different from the one we enjoy now," reflected Roland. "It makes me wonder if this might be the last quiet meal the three of us enjoy together before we are swept away on an adventure of our own."

I wanted desperately to ask Roland what he meant, what would come on the gathering wind, where it might lead us the very next day. But something told me he wouldn't reveal anything even if I asked, and that if I would only listen, the answer would be waiting at the end of his story.

And so, on that magical moonlit night, I held a hot cup of tea in my hand and did not speak. Instead I listened as Roland Warvold led me out into the wild world of the Great Ravine with Thomas and Thorn at his side.

CHAPTER 14

A Thousand Stingers

In the excitement of all that had happened the night before, there hadn't been time to sleep or eat. We'd had a little to drink on the raft while crossing over the Lake of Fire, but that had been all we'd enjoyed. So it should come as no surprise that two young boys, after having eaten what little they had, began to feel sleepy. There were a few words, then Thomas and I both went from sitting to leaning back on our elbows, and then, without warning, we were both lying down, trying to stay awake, but completely out of energy. I don't know if Thorn slept as we did, but I have to imagine that she at least nodded off from time to time.

After a while Thomas woke, poking my side and yawning.

"What? Who's there?" were my first words. Then, rubbing my eyes, I asked, "How long have we been asleep?"

"It's getting on late afternoon. You've both slept the morning and most of the day away," answered Thorn.

I could hardly believe we'd been asleep so long, and right away I was aware of how thirsty and hungry I was.

"Is there anywhere to get water or food in the Great Ravine?" asked Thomas, sounding as though he felt the same way I did. "We haven't had much of either in a while."

Thorn got up and began to walk toward the entrance to the cave. "Bring the bag with the jug, and follow me as quietly as you can. Lots of noise won't do."

We had no idea how long our journey to water and food would last when it began, and had we known, I'm sure we would have gone back to sleep and forgotten we'd awakened at all. The long, narrow trail that led along the edge of the cliffs descended at a steep grade. And it went on and on and on. About an hour after we began, a breeze kicked up that soon turned into a howling wind, whipping the dust up into our eyes and our mouths. No one spoke, and when we coughed or tried to clear our throats, Thorn turned back to us with a glare that communicated what she'd already told us: *Lots of noise won't do!*

I kept looking around, trying to imagine who or what could possibly hear us through the blinding wind. We were utterly alone on the narrow trail, and I could only imagine that those who lived in the Great Ravine could hear a whole lot better than I could.

We came near the bottom and Thorn stopped, staring all along the bottom of the ravine, her ears pointing hard and straight to the sky. The wind began to fade and soon it was half the strength it had been on our descent.

"We can speak now," she purred. "Though still in whispers."

There were questions upon questions running through my head, but Thomas was faster at opening his mouth than I was. His voice sounded dry and cracked.

"How will we get out of the ravine once we're at the very bottom, at the deepest part?" he asked.

"It's the only way, I'm afraid. The only way to get what Mister Clawson wants," Thorn replied.

"I thought you said he wasn't your master," I interrupted, surprised by my own boldness.

Thorn glanced at me with a strange expression I didn't understand.

"If I don't bring back what he wants, it will be the two of you he will punish the most. We'd best not go back at all if we can't do what we're told."

"That's exactly it!" cried Thomas.

"Lower your voice!" Thorn purred emphatically. "I know it seems there is no one and nothing to fear. But they're near, and we must be careful not to arouse their attention."

I was curious what she meant, but there was a point I'd wanted to make all along and I couldn't wait any longer to express it.

"Thorn, you don't understand — we don't *want* to go back," I started, but she didn't let me finish. The wind had died down to almost nothing as we spoke. Her ears were again perked up and listening.

"Follow me!" she whispered. "And no more talking. This is our chance!"

Thomas and I looked at each other, wishing we could speak. But Thorn was already ahead of us, moving swiftly down the last of the narrow path. We shrugged at each other and began to move again. There was a sound in the air — a sound that had a familiar ring to it, but I couldn't place what it was or from where it was coming.

Reaching the bottom of the path, Thorn broke into a run. There were huge rocks jutting up all around us, and we tried to keep up with her through the twisting maze of towering stone and desert earth. The sound was getting louder and suddenly I *could* place it. It was buzzing, a steady, distant buzzing.

"Open up the bag!" growled Thorn. We had come around the side of a gigantic red stone the size of Madame Vickers's house. The stone extended out at

129

the middle over open air, and Thorn stood beneath it looking at us impatiently.

"There's no time," she said. "Open the bag and come quickly!"

I took the bag off my shoulder and undid the straps as fast as I could. We were under the overhanging stone, and the sound of buzzing was growing louder.

"Most of them are away, but there are still some that remain," said Thorn. Directly above her there was a hole the size of my head, and out of the hole came a bee that was bigger than any bee I'd seen before. It was as long as my smallest finger, as fat as my thumb, and as it flew away I saw a stinger that took my breath away. Thomas was standing next to Thorn, watching the bees emerge from the hole like a dripping faucet. First there was one, then ten, then fifty. But they seemed not to notice us as they dribbled out of the hole in ones and twos and flew off around the giant rock.

"We've got only a moment before our chance is lost," said Thorn. "Bring me the bag. Thomas, you must put your hand inside and break off whatever you can get your hands on."

"Will they sting me?" he asked.

Thorn answered hesitantly, "They might."

"We don't need it!" I screamed, suddenly aghast at the idea of Thomas putting his hand inside the hole. Thorn shot me a glance that was dreadfully clear in its meaning. *Now you've done it. Why couldn't you just keep quiet like I asked?*

Without warning Thomas thrust his hand into the hole. He whimpered, and I could see that he'd been stung once, maybe twice. But he gritted his teeth, cursed a word he'd heard at the Ainsworth orphanage, and pulled his hand out. Within the grasp of his fingers was a large chunk of honeycomb that glowed yellow with dripping honey.

"Put it in the bag!" Thorn roared. "And run! Run as fast as you can!"

Thorn darted past me, followed by Thomas, who dropped the honeycomb in the bag as he went by. The sound of buzzing, which had been far off, now seemed to be growing steadily nearer.

"Roland!" screamed Thorn. "Come on!"

I was terrified and didn't realize I hadn't even moved. I'd been stung by bees at the House on the Hill and hated the hot pain when it happened. The idea of a thousand impossibly long stingers piercing my skin had frozen my mind and my legs. It took Thorn's voice to bring me back to life. I dashed off in the direction of her voice faster than I'd ever run before.

Not far off I could see that we were coming to the end of the Great Ravine. It ended like a V, getting narrower and narrower until there was nothing left but a thin line of stone extending into the sky above. I looked back over my shoulder and to my horror saw that the buzzing sound came from a vast swarm of bees. It was a menacing red cloud descending on us — filled with thousands upon thousands of gigantic, swarming, angry insects. It was the most horrible kind of nightmare for a boy of ten.

"This way!" cried Thomas. "Keep running!"

Thorn circled and darted back toward me. I'd fallen farther behind than I could have imagined as I looked ahead and saw Thomas waving me on from the distance. I expected Thorn to come alongside me and prod me along with her powerful voice, so it came as a surprise when she kept running toward me at full speed. It seemed as though she might keep going and flash past me toward the oncoming swarm, but that was not to be, for I'd fallen too far behind.

"Down on the ground!" she cried. "Get down on the ground! You're too close!"

Purely by instinct I did what I was told, running into a dive and bouncing off the earth in a heap. I looked back from where I lay and realized the mighty swarm of giant bees was about to overtake me. There was only time for a fleeting glimpse at Thorn as the maddening sound of bees descended from the sky, but in that brief moment I witnessed the great mountain lion — all six feet and two hundred pounds of gray cat — leaping into the air. She came down directly on top of me and settled onto the ground — encircling me in her powerful legs, neck, and head — until I was utterly smothered in a thick blanket of fur. Her head was near mine. I heard her whispering as the swarm attacked: *Don't worry. It will be over soon. Stay very still.*

I heard something else that made me feel terrible, a sound I will never forget. Even with her thick coat, the angry swarm of bees were able to get through and sting, sting, sting. I heard Thorn try to hold back any sound, but it was impossible to hide the fact that a thousand stingers were leaving their mark on this brave new friend of mine. One of the bees found its way through and crawled down into my old black boot, and when I felt the sting I knew a tiny part of what Thorn was enduring on my behalf. A voice in my head began ringing. *If only I hadn't stopped; if only I could have kept up. If only. If only.* I felt true regret and wished with all my heart that I could turn back the clock a few small minutes and run faster.

I don't know how long the swarm stayed — my mind racing as it did. I only remember finding it suddenly quiet, the sound of buzzing bees drifting off. They had made us pay for the honeycomb, and I imagined them all laughing as they returned to their work.

I didn't move – I didn't want to face what would come next – until Thomas was over us yelling my name and rolling Thorn off to the side.

"Roland! Roland! Are you all right?"

"I'm fine," I murmured, looking off into the sky and seeing the swarm was far, far away, moving up the wall of the canyon. I turned my attention to Thorn. She was lying on her side, completely still, her eyes half open and dreamy.

"Thorn," I whispered. "I'm so sorry I didn't keep up. I've made a terrible mistake."

She didn't move, but she seemed to smile, licking her nose and coming to life little by little. She raised her head and my heart leaped. Could it really be so? Could she be all right?

A moment later she was up, wobbling uneasily.

"That didn't feel very good," she joked, shaking her head from side to side. "Let's try not to let it happen again, understood?"

Both Thomas and I threw our arms around Thorn, digging our faces into her neck and smiling from ear to ear. We didn't think at all about her sharp claws or long teeth. We were past being afraid of her now, and only wanted Thorn to know how much we needed her. She purred thankfully, which tickled my ear and made me pull back.

"Everything is a little sore to the touch," she said, gently suggesting we hold off on any further acts of affection until all the stings had time to heal. She walked around on shaking legs and seemed agitated and uncertain.

"The sooner we get out of the Great Ravine and back to Mister Clawson, the better," she said. "We don't want to find ourselves lost in the wild after dark. Best to start back now."

"Could we rest a while longer?" asked Thomas. "I saw something back there, something we need to talk about." He gestured toward the very bottom of the Great Ravine, where the two sides of the long cavernous V met and the black line of rock shot up into the air.

Thorn looked inquisitively at Thomas, then back toward the wide open of the rest of the ravine. She smelled the air, licked at her nose, then squinted her eyes as if trying to see what danger might be heading our way.

"A *very* short rest will be all right," she conceded. "But only a few minutes, and let's move back as far as we can, where we can't be seen."

The three of us wandered back between the scattered rocks of deep brown and red, until we

135

came to the end. It was there that I saw what Thomas had already seen. At the end of the Great Ravine was a hidden passage, narrow and black as night, rising fast and crooked like the long tail of a lightning bolt. And on a large flat stone that lay before the opening was carved the circle and square symbol – the very symbol that could be found on my knees, hidden beneath my dusty pants.

CHAPTER 15

A Fateful Decision
Is Made

"Someone must want you to go that way," said Thorn. Thomas and I had sat down, rolled up our pant legs, and revealed the marks above our knees. Thorn looked back and forth between the symbol on the stone before the passage and the matching symbol permanently marked into our skin.

"How can that be?" she wondered.

"We've wanted to tell you," said Thomas. "But we weren't sure we could trust you. We thought you might want to put an end to us — that Mister Clawson had sent us out here to die. Before we knew you, we feared you would slash us to bits and leave us out here in the Great Ravine once we got what Mister Clawson wanted."

There was a pause, a lingering moment of indecision for my brother. He pointed to the image on my knee. "We've been called out onto a journey we don't understand. These markings mean something."

It's hard to tell what a big cat is thinking by

137

looking her in the face, but I saw something in Thorn then, in her eyes mostly. She was afraid, like a child is afraid. She didn't know what to do.

"Do you know where you came from?" Thomas softly whispered. "Long ago you came from the forest and the mountains, from somewhere up there." Thomas pointed up the passage hidden in shadows. "That's where we want to go. You could join us – protect us if you would – and you'll never have to see Mister Clawson again."

Thorn's eyes brightened – but only for a moment. Then her mood turned dim and lonely.

"We must go back," she told us. "We *must* bring Mister Clawson what he requires. You're wrong to think we can escape his grasp. He has his ways, and he'll put them to use if we try to escape him."

"What *ways*?" I said. "You don't need to worry over leaving us in the Great Ravine to die. We're not staying here. We're going that way, to the Western Kingdom."

I glanced off toward the passageway, rolling my pant legs down and standing up. Thorn seemed completely flustered by the idea that we'd want to travel so far – and through such dangerous places – but she said nothing.

"He's had you under his control since you were a cub," I continued. "What could he possibly have said to make you think you couldn't escape him?"

She paced back and forth with uncertainty, her mind racing with what to do.

"It's dangerous out there for two children," she said. "There are bears and wolves, and they know easy prey when they see it. Where you seek to go is beyond the wild of Fenwick Forest, beyond even Mount Norwood . . ."

Her voice trailed off, and it was clear she'd come to the name of her old home, distant memories clouding her mind.

"We *have* to go, Thorn," I said. "But we need you to come with us. We can't do it alone."

This seemed to crack Thorn's resolve, though something still troubled her. She listened carefully on the wind, trying to sense any oncoming danger, but there was nothing. After a long pause she began to speak in a quiet, cheerless voice.

"When I was small, my mother told me a story about a little bear cub that was captured by a man and taken away. The man tied the cub with a rope to a stake in the ground and the cub tried and tried to break free. After a while the cub gave up and the man trained it to do tricks. He lived at the edge of a large town where people threw coins at the man and the bear, and always the cub was tied to the rope attached to the stake in the ground."

Thorn stopped and listened, sniffing the air for coming intruders.

"When the cub grew into a bear, it was much bigger than the man, much stronger," she went on. "But still the man kept the bear tied to the same flimsy rope tied to the same wooden stake pounded into the ground. The grown bear could have easily broken free if he had tried, but he had come to believe over the course of time that it could not be broken. The man had trained the bear's mind to think it couldn't break free, and so the bear lived until it was very old, tied to the rope, doing tricks for anyone who passed by."

"What happened to the bear?" I asked, saddened by the story but wanting to get to the point so that we could escape the Great Ravine.

"There was a young girl who saw the bear and felt sorry for it. This girl came in the night and cut the rope while the bear lay sleeping. The bear awoke with a start, seeing the rope had been cut."

"So the bear escaped then," said Thomas. "It ran off in the night and found its way home."

"No," said Thorn. "The bear looked all around and, not knowing what to do, woke his master and showed him the rope. Now the master knew he had trained the bear well. From that day forward, there was no rope, no stake, nothing to keep the bear at his master's side. And yet the bear never tried to leave. He died of loneliness, clutching the old cut rope at night like a child's blanket, wishing for the courage to leave."

"That's a very sad story," I said. "Why do you think your mother told it to you?"

"So I would never wander off and be captured, I suppose," said Thorn. "But my mother knew my headstrong nature. She knew I might roam into places I shouldn't go. Maybe she wanted me to know that if ever I was captured, the rope that held me was a lie, and that if I chose, I could escape."

"It's never too late to stop believing a lie," said Thomas. "You need only courage and friends, and you have both."

Thorn looked at Thomas and then at me. Neither of us could be sure what she was thinking. A long silence fell between us, until it was broken by an approaching, violent sound.

We had stayed too long in the Great Ravine.

"That will be much worse than the swarm of bees if it reaches us," Thorn warned, clearly alarmed. "There's not a lot of food down here, and the two of you would make a nice dinner for a pack of hungry wolves."

I felt a deep fear returning at the thought of wild animals tearing me apart, but Thomas seemed unmoved as he looked at Thorn. "Come with us," he said. "You can go back home, to the forest and the mountains where you belong, and Mister Clawson will never find you."

"The wolves are near," said Thorn, sniffing the air. "We have no choice but to make our way out of the Great Ravine."

Thomas smiled at Thorn's decision. He was most comfortable on a grand adventure, and it appeared that this one would continue deeper into the wild, to places we'd heard of but never seen. With the growing sound of wolves at our back we started into the narrow passage with Thorn close behind. I imagined the bellowing sound of Mister Clawson's voice becoming quieter and quieter the farther we climbed, up and away from his grasp.

THROUGH
UNCHARTED LANDS

"I do not think it serves my story very well to tell you all of what happened on the journey from the Great Ravine through Fenwick Forest and into the realm of Mount Norwood," Roland told me and Yipes. The hour was getting late, but I was anything but sleepy. "So I will give a brief account of our passage to the Western Kingdom and the mystery of the Wakefield House awaiting us there."

"You will tell us something about Fenwick Forest and Mount Norwood in the olden days, won't you?" chirped Yipes. He'd been so quiet in the dark that I'd begun to wonder if he'd nodded off. I should have known he was only listening carefully, waiting on every word.

"It's getting on ten o'clock," said Roland, looking up into the sky, observing the stars. He took out his logbook and pen, scribbling something short and fast in the margin of a tattered page. "If we are to reach the end of this tale before we all have fallen asleep, I really must keep things moving along. However, I will not fail to give you a brief and colorful view of our journey through uncharted lands."

The wind had not returned, and there was a single candle sitting between us, its light bobbing softly over the wood of the deck. It was reflected in Roland's piercing eyes, and I sat up straight, unwilling to allow myself to grow sleepy and miss anything the old man of the sea might share with us. There seemed to be some reason for him to have chosen this night, some reason why he felt the whole story needed to be told before darkness passed into the light of morning. As if we might see something then that we would only understand in the telling of the tale.

"It was a long while before we found our way out of the Great Ravine. Day was like night in the deep and narrow crevice which held us, and there were times when the passageway became so thin we thought of turning back. The wolves had come only a little way in, howling angrily at missing a rare chance to capture such a fine dinner as two boys lost in the wilderness. There were places where we needed to climb and pull one another up, places where sharp corners turned us back and forth against jagged stones. All along the way, water trickled at our feet, and here and there we found small pools to drink from. Everything was damp and cold as we rose higher. Moss began to appear as we came nearer to the top and light wafted into the passage from above. There was plenty to drink, which kept us going, and we had the honeycomb in the bag. We broke off clumps and ate ravenously, and by the time we approached the top half, the honeycomb was gone."

"What did you find when you came out into Fenwick Forest? Was it the same as it is today?" broke in Yipes.

He was very curious about the forest and what it had been like.

"This was a time before people had been into Fenwick Forest," said Roland. "It's quite possible that Thomas and I were only the second and third people to travel that way. As we entered the forest it certainly felt as though we were unwelcome, like we'd stumbled into a place we should not have come."

"Wait a minute," Yipes interrupted. "The second and the third? But who was the first to enter the forest?"

Roland smiled wryly. "Whoever left the circle and square images for us to follow."

"Who was that? Who do you mean?"

Roland took great satisfaction in his answer:

"Who indeed."

Yipes made a long *hmmmmmmmm* sound, carried away by the idea of who might have come before.

"We had a bit of good fortune there in the forest that made our passage less difficult than it might have been," Roland continued. "We weren't an hour into the towering trees and the sound of birds chirping all around us when Thorn told us to stop and remain very still. We listened carefully but heard nothing, and then Thorn motioned for us to continue on. There was something near, though I couldn't imagine what it was. I could *feel* it, big and deadly in our midst. We came through the trees into a rocky clearing, and Thorn looked off to one side, our gaze following hers. There, only a few feet away and standing on a large,

round rock, was a gigantic grizzly bear. He growled fero-
ciously, making his presence known to everything in the
forest. There were no words and yet I understood, like I
understood Thorn, by the sound of the bear's angry voice
and the whipping back and forth of his huge head.

"'You know not to bring them here. Why have you
done this wicked thing?' the bear roared. We were even
more unwelcome than I had imagined. It sounded as
though the bear would sooner bat us to the ground with its
claws than let us retreat back into the Great Ravine from
which we'd come.

"As Thorn and the bear spoke, Thomas and I listened.
The bear was the Forest King of a time now long forgotten.
Thorn told him of our plight and of her own capture by
Mister Clawson so many years ago. As a gesture, she
offered what remained of our honeycomb if only the great
bear would let us pass through. The Forest King approached
us, sniffing our hair so close I could smell his breath of pine
and berries. It was the scariest moment of our journey so
far, the powerful jaws of a grizzly close enough to chomp
down on our necks.

"But the Forest King was touched by Thorn's story
and intrigued by the prospect of honeycomb from the
Great Ravine, for every bear loves sugary treats and honeycomb the very most. I took the honeycomb from my
pack, sticky and heavy with sweetness, and I held it out.
'Put it down,' said the Forest King, and so I did. My hand
was sticky, and the great bear licked it clean with a coarse

tongue the size of my grown foot. I laughed nervously from the tickle on my hand and watched as the Forest King lay down and began working at the honeycomb, mumbling happily to himself."

I licked my lips on the salty sea air and looked over at Yipes, who was doing the same. Roland had made the honeycomb sound so sweet and tasty it was hard not to want some for ourselves.

"So he let you pass?" I asked.

"He did more than that," answered Roland. "He walked with us for three days, showing us the way we should go, warning off predators. Thorn told him the story her mother had told — about the bear tied to the rope — and this made the Forest King very sad and reflective. He told us again and again that he was only taking us through so that there would be no trace of humans in Fenwick Forest. 'If I kill you here in the forest, some part of you will remain, but if I take you through to the other side and let you free, it will be as though you were never here.' He was convinced that having us out of the forest entirely would be better than having us dead within it. Thomas and I were afraid even to relieve ourselves along the way, and had to sneak off to one side or wait until the Forest King slept to do our business in secret.

"When we reached the end of the forest that sat at the foot of Mount Norwood, the Forest King turned to us with a graveness not unlike that which we'd seen when we'd first come upon him and given up our honeycomb. 'A time is coming when humans will enter the wild and kill the magic,' he said. 'You won't understand me then, so listen to me now. Stay away from Fenwick Forest. You will be sorry if we cross paths again.' And then he left us all alone, his enormous shoulders rising and falling as if in slow motion as he stepped away through the trees.

"We were on our way into the mountains, into the realm of the mountain lion. From the very start, there was something different about this place. There was a feeling of being watched in a way I had never felt before. It felt as though we were tracked by something much bigger than ourselves, something even larger than the giant bear. Whatever it was remained close but unseen, following us like we were prey — and waiting until it was ready to attack us.

"Our journey quickened on the second day, near the top of the mountain. At all times, Thorn seemed to know the way we should go. It was as if she had entered into a place that sparked a hidden knowledge, opening her memory to a time before the rope and the stake in the ground of Mister Clawson's home.

"Higher and higher we went, feeding on the wild berries and drinking from the crackling clear streams. It was cooler next to the water and we stayed near its edge or walked right in and splashed one another, which Thorn found annoying. She was not the sort of cat who appreciated getting very wet, and so we cooled ourselves and she kept our pace a few feet off.

"We never went to the very top of Mount Norwood, though we came very near to it. There came a moment when Thorn suggested we'd gone high enough, and she turned to the side, away from the stream we followed, into tougher terrain. The ground filled with underbrush and the trees thinned out. It was hotter away from the stream, and we complained as boys will do, but Thorn would not waver in her resolve to head us in the direction she'd chosen.

"After hours of walking through low brush and wild-flowers, we came to an aspen grove. It seemed to pop up out of nowhere, a whole world of long white trunks speck-led with black and brown and topped with bright green leaves. There was a slight breeze on the air and the million tiny leaves danced and sang as we entered the grove. It was instantly cooler then, with the leaves overhead and the cool white of the rising white trunks all around us.

"'We have come to the very end,' said Thorn. Another mountain lion must have heard her purring voice, for a moment later we heard a roar. We could hear something bounding through the trees, coming toward us, and we began to run out of the aspen grove and down the moun-tain. I remember running in front of my brother and seeing the thing that stopped us before he did. We had darted off at our fastest, and found a mountain lion even bigger than Thorn standing in our path. I tried to slow down and change course, but Thomas was close behind. He tumbled into me and we both fell in a pile on the ground. When we looked up, it became clear that we wouldn't be running away whether we wanted to or not.

"There were three mountain lions standing in a circle around us. One was Thorn, who had come down the hill after us. Standing beside her was an older, slightly smaller mountain lion. And then there was the third — the one that had stopped us in our tracks — and this one was bigger and fiercer than the other two put together.

"'Thomas and Roland,' Thorn said. Her voice was shaking and there was something new in the look on her face — something magical — as if she'd found her way home after a long and perilous journey. 'Meet my father.' She nodded toward the hulking beast that stood over us, then looked at the creature standing next to her. 'And this is my mother.'

"Tears of happiness were shed and stories were told in the aspen grove that day. It is a cherished memory, the first time in my life I felt as though I had the power to change things for good. *Me* — an orphaned boy picking garbage at Madame Vickers's House on the Hill — *I* could change someone's life and make it better if only I had the courage and the will to do it. That day in the aspen grove changed my life — changed Thomas's life — in a new and profound way. Before then we had lived only for the adventure in the journey, for the sights and sounds and thrills of discovering the wild and hidden places of The Land of Elyon. But from that point on — all the way through Thomas's life, and through mine on the *Warwick Beacon* — our adventure came from abandoning ourselves to the desperate needs of others. And this, more than anything, gave us happiness."

"It must have been something else to see Thorn with her mother and father again after so long," I said quietly. Roland, the battered old man of the Lonely Sea, turned away and I had to wonder if he was wiping away a tear.

"A terrible childhood like the one Thomas and I endured can be redeemed," he said over his shoulder, "if only we can hold on to a few good memories. A few moments of joy overcome a thousand lonely nights at sea."

Sitting on the deck of the *Warwick Beacon*, I could imagine how thoughts such as Thorn's release from captivity and reunion with her parents could keep Roland going through untold days and nights at sea, even if he was made to take the journey alone.

"And now we turn to the Wakefield House and the great mystery it revealed to me," said Roland.

"Wait just a minute." Yipes, quiet and reflective up to that point, was suddenly alert and questioning. "You can't jump all the way down the side of the mountain and out of the wild just like that. That's not fair! What about Thorn? What happened to her?"

"She was home, and we were but a day's journey from our destination," said Roland. "We needed only to make our way down the side of Mount Norwood and walk along the cliffs at the edge of the Lonely Sea. We stayed on in the aspen grove for a night and a morning, but it wouldn't have been right for us to stay there longer than that. And besides, we were eager to find the Western Kingdom and see the Wakefield House. Thorn and her parents walked with us down the mountain, but when we reached the bottom it was time for us to part ways. There was no question that Thorn would stay home. She had waited too long to return to it."

There was a silence in the night as Yipes and I both thought about leaving Thorn behind. It was one of the troubles with journeys and adventures — we were always finding new friends and leaving others behind in the wake of our movements. I came to realize something then that I hadn't thought of before. Someday I would have to stop leaving and start staying, or I might find myself old and gray with an exciting life behind me and no one to remember it with on a porch with a cup of tea. It was something of a curse — this need for always going farther, deeper into the wild. I wondered if I would someday outgrow it.

"Did you ever see Thorn again?" I asked.

"I did not," said Roland. "But I see her every day in my memory. I see her standing at the foot of the mountains, restored to her parents and her home. She said she would watch over us, from a distance, and that she would never forget what we'd done for her. And I do feel her watching over me, sheltering me as she once did on that first perilous journey into the wild. Without her, the rest of our story would have gone unwritten."

Roland sat down upon a three-legged stool we'd brought out for him hours ago.

"Her spirit remains," he concluded, "ever watching, ever protecting an old man at sea."

"I'm ready then," said Yipes, surprising both Roland and me with his quick and unexpected resolve. "Let's leave her behind if we must, but do go on with the story. I'm wide-awake and it's so still on the water tonight. You *must* tell us the rest. You must tell us right now!"

"How right you are," said Roland, laughing momentarily at the enthusiasm of our companion. "I must tell you the rest before dawn comes to the Lonely Sea, whether you like it or not."

CHAPTER 17

The Wakefield House

As we drew farther away along the cliffs, I felt Thorn watching us from somewhere atop the mountain, and I felt that other set of eyes watching us — the ones that were larger and scarier — from somewhere in the hidden realm of the wild. Whatever it was had stopped moving with us, and it seemed as if it was watching us from a hidden place in our past, not wanting us to escape into a new day. For a long time I had wondered when it would choose to pounce on us. Now, with the feeling of its presence weakening on each step out of the mountains, I began to think the feeling of being watched had been only a dramatic figment of my imagination. As much as I'd loved the thrill of our flight through Fenwick Forest and over Mount Norwood, I was glad to be free of this unseen fear that had haunted our movements.

Out in the open along the cliffs it seemed far less wild, as though we were at a threshold between the tamed and the untamed world. We'd come only a short distance away from the base of the mountain and were without Thorn to protect us. Thomas and I walked that way and stopped many times so that he could paint pictures of what he saw. He painted the forest and mountains from memory and the clouds over the Lonely Sea and the Dark Hills off in the distance. From that point on, he was most fond of using a brush made from Thorn's fur rather than any from the children at the House on the Hill.

"You'd better slow down," I said, watching him busy at his work. "If you keep it up you might run out of pages."

He scowled at me, but he knew it was true and couldn't help flipping his fingers through the remaining pages of the journal . . . as if he didn't already know the exact number that remained. He put his things away and looked off in the direction we were heading.

"Do you see that?" he said, pocketing his journal and box of supplies.

"What?" I didn't know what he was talking about.

"Don't you see it there? That tall thing. It's the same color as the things behind it, but it sticks up high in the air."

I still couldn't see what he meant, and thought he might be either making it up to play a trick on me or seeing some sort of mirage in the rising heat of the morning. But as we walked on I, too, began to see the extraordinarily high, thin structure in the distance, as well as the small houses scattered at its base.

The Western Kingdom was before us, and we couldn't help but believe that the tall spire that rose into the sky was the Wakefield House. We had come at last to the place we'd been searching for.

We quickened our pace and talked nervously about what we would do when we arrived at the edge of town. I was convinced we should wait until dark, then go in for a look around. But Thomas didn't understand the logic of such an idea.

"Why would we want to do that?" he asked. "We're so far from home, nobody will have a clue where we've come from. We've endured a lake of fire, a swarm of giant bees, a pack of hungry wolves, and a monstrous bear, not to mention all the blisters on my feet. I'm going right in there. You can stay back if you want."

Of course, I wasn't about to stay behind and let him go alone. His mind was made up, and I knew better than to try and change it. So we walked the rest of the way with a heightened exhilaration, knowing we were about to stand at the foot of the Wakefield House. We stopped only once, about a quarter of a mile from the Western Kingdom, so that Thomas could paint the rising house from a distance. It was an extraordinary sight, as much for its height as its location. The Western Kingdom, it turned out, had been improperly named, probably by someone living there who wished it were worthy of such a title. It would be hard to refer to this place we'd stumbled upon as a town, let alone a kingdom, because once you got past the grandeur of the Wakefield House there wasn't much of anything else to see. It was like looking at a single gray tree trunk soaring into the sky, surrounded by a scattered collection of pebbles and dirt clods at its base.

When Thomas was finished painting, we quietly walked the last of the cliff-side trail into the Western Kingdom, watching the Wakefield House get taller and taller as we went. There was no gate to pass through, and I noticed right away there couldn't have been more than a hundred stone houses in all. There were no cobblestone streets, only dirt pathways with cart-wheel gutters worn into them.

There was a horse tied to a fence post outside the first house we came to, and there was a woman sitting in its doorway eating something soft, squishy, and yellow out of a bowl. She looked up at us uninterestedly and spoke as if we were nothing special.

"Come a long way, did you?" she asked, slurping some of the contents of the bowl from her spoon. My stomach growled.

"A very long way," answered Thomas, saying the words in a way that conveyed a craving for something to eat. "We've come to look at the Wakefield House."

"Figured as much," the woman said. "Same reason everyone else comes here."

She had a detached way about her, as if she'd endured this conversation before, and we weren't making it any more interesting than the last time she'd had it. My stomach growled again, and she looked up from her bowl.

"You might as well come over here and get some soup," she offered. "It looks like you two have been living on berries and river water and not much else."

I wasn't entirely sure I wanted what the woman was offering, but she'd spoken the truth about our recent breakfast, lunch, and dinner. Anything at this point would be better than a bowl of berries. She stepped through her front door and acted like she expected us to follow her.

"If you want something to eat, you'll have to come inside," she said. "That's the way it works."

Thomas barely hesitated before making his way past the horse, down the very short path that lay before the house, and through the door. I reluctantly followed, though I had a feeling we were making a mistake following someone we didn't know into a house we'd never seen before.

"Mine's the first house people find in their search for the Wakefield House," she said, dropping a ladle into a small pot sitting on a table and pouring the thick soup off into two bowls. I didn't want to say it, but it looked an awful lot like the stuff Thomas blew out of his nose in the morning without the aide of a handkerchief, aiming for a tree and laughing his head off while everyone around him including me cried *eeeeeewwwww*.

We took the bowls and the spoons, and Thomas — always the more reckless between the two of us — had the spoon filled and into his mouth before I'd finished giving the yellowy, thick soup a good sniff.

"Saaaaaaay," he said, drawing out the word as he filled his spoon again. "This is very good."

"Better be," said the woman. "I got the recipe from a well-to-do chef who traveled all the way over here from the Northern Kingdoms to try his luck at the Wakefield House."

There was a deep pause, and then she said something more.

"He failed, just like all the rest."

I slurped up a spoonful of soup and couldn't help letting out a soft *mmmmmmm*. It was creamy and sweet, with a tang at the end that made me smack my lips as I drew another spoonful out of the bowl. I looked at the woman across the table and found that it was hard to say how old she was. She was of a sort that no matter her age you couldn't help imagining what she'd looked like when she was nine or ten. She had the bright eyes and pug nose of a child, but the crow's feet and graying temples of a woman of fifty or more. She wore a white, sunny-looking dress that left her long brown arms bare. They were arms of summer, of days in the garden baked by the heat.

"Why did he give you the recipe?" my brother asked. It was a logical question, one that had eluded me for some unknown reason as I gulped down spoonful after spoonful of the wonderful soup.

"When you fail to find the top of the Wakefield House, there is a price to pay," she said. Then, after a slow slurp of her own and a drawn-out pause, she added, "I set the price, and the price for the chef was his most secret recipe, one that had been handed down to him by his mother and her mother before, one that was a family treasure of great worth. The only recipe he wasn't supposed to share with anyone. That's the kind of price I like."

The image of the paper we'd found on the hill of garbage flashed in my mind.

Western Kingdom — Wakefield House — Miss Flannery — FAILED!

"You don't by any chance know of a woman named Miss Flannery?" I asked. "We're looking for her, because of a piece of paper we found back home."

The woman reached behind her and pulled a piece of paper off a stack an inch high. It was in the form of a certificate, clean and laced with gold ink. The same four words and the circle and square image we'd seen on the piece of paper from the hill were now before us on the table.

"I'm Miss Flannery," she said, holding out the paper. "Was the sheet you saw one of these by any chance?" she asked.

"It was," I answered. "We found it in a saddle-bag attached to an old dead horse. The saddlebag had the name Mingleton branded onto it."

"Mingleton?" she asked, very nearly sounding interested . . . but not quite. "I remember Mingleton. That was years ago."

She went back to her soup. It was maddening how she remained so detached, so uninterested.

"So he tried to reach the top of the Wakefield house, but failed?" asked Thomas, trying to draw her out once more.

"He did," said Miss Flannery, flipping a chain

161

around her neck up and out from under her dress to reveal a bright blue stone as big as my thumb.

"Miner Mingleton," said Miss Flannery.

"Miner?" asked Thomas. We were both staring at the incredibly large and beautiful stone dangling from her neck.

"That's what he called himself, Miner Mingleton," she continued. "He went into the deepest caves he could locate in search of rare stones. He discovered many, but this was his greatest find. It's a star sapphire. You see how it makes a six-pronged starlight at the center?"

She held the sapphire and moved it ever so slightly back and forth. There really was a bright white star gleaming inside.

"This was his price," she said, tucking it back under her dress.

I looked around the room more carefully now, wondering how many of the objects were things that someone had once cherished, but were now lost to the Wakefield House. There were a lot of valuable-looking things on the shelves around the small room — books, artifacts, vases, paintings. It made the room look less like a home and more like a museum of stolen treasures.

"Why don't they just leave and take their possessions with them? These things you have, they don't seem to be well protected," said Thomas. I was aware as he said it that she was not a very fierce-looking woman. There were no weapons and the door remained wide open.

This seemed to amuse Miss Flannery, for her lip curled up on one corner ever so slightly and her eyes twinkled.

"Some have tried such a trick on me," she said slyly, letting the words hang in the air. "None have succeeded."

I wanted to ask why no one could betray her, but she was a mysterious and oddly frightening woman, and I didn't get the feeling she would tell us anything more. Her words were enough to scare me into thinking two boys from Madame Vickers's House on the Hill were no match for her.

I heard Thomas's spoon clang against the bottom of his bowl. Looking down, I realized that his bowl was not the only one that was sadly empty. I managed to scrape one more half bite off the bottom, and then the soup was gone.

"Follow me," said Miss Flannery. She stood up and walked out the door, down the path, and past the horse tied to the post. We followed her, passing houses with gardens for front yards and people busy at work or play. They were as cool as Miss Flannery, looking up without interest and returning to whatever it was they were doing without much hesitation.

When we reached the door to the Wakefield House, she turned and stood motionless while Thomas and I craned our necks into the sky, trying to find the top of the towering structure. The supremacy of its height was alarming, doubled by the closeness of the slabs of stone and beams of wood rising from the ground. It was not a pretty structure, and lacked the feel of something made by a craftsman. There was a hastiness to its design, as though it might topple over at any moment from the sheer weight of itself. And yet, there was also something brilliant about the completeness of it. The parts were crude — chunks of stone and blocks of wood — but the whole was astonishingly solid and intricate. It was at once a profound masterpiece and a reckless pile of rubble.

Thomas started for the door, overcome by the power of the moment and dying to get inside. There was no fear in him, no concern that the Wakefield House might topple over while we were inside or that we might become hopelessly lost in its winding interior. My thoughts ran to more practical matters, such as the total lack of success for all who'd faced the Wakefield House before us, and the fact that we were going nowhere until we gave Miss Flannery our most prized possession. I knew what the possession was, but I wasn't sure Thomas did,

164

and this worried me as I watched him advance toward the door.

"You're going the wrong way." Miss Flannery said this in such a way that it made me think she had said the same words to a hundred visitors already and was mildly annoyed at having to say them again. "That's the way out, not the way in. In all my years as the keeper of the Wakefield House, that door has never been opened."

She walked up next to Thomas, and I followed. As I came closer, I realized that it was an iron door, shaped in much the same way as the iron door that led away from Mister Clawson's lair. A chill ran through me as we got to Thomas on the dirt path.

"It only opens from the inside," Miss Flannery explained, "and no one — including me — has ever made it anywhere near this door from the other side."

The whole affair was beginning to sound like a very bad idea to me, and I was about to tell Thomas we should sit back and think it through before proceeding, but I was too late. Thomas already had our most prized possession out in the open, holding it out to Miss Flannery.

"What's this?" she asked, taking the objects from Thomas with uncharacteristic interest. When it came to the cost of entering the Wakefield House, she was at once full of curiosity.

"The box has my brushes and glue and powders to make colors. The journal has my paintings and my notes. Our whole lives are in there — everything we've seen and done — it's all there in pictures and scribbles."

She flipped open the small wooden box and looked inside, carefully touching the bags of dried flowers and dust, running her finger across the myriad colors on the inside of the lid. Closing the box, she opened to the first page of the journal and studied it. A smile grew on her face as she went to the second page, then the third. She was engrossed in the tiny paintings, lost in the world of my brother's making.

"You may go," she said without looking up from the page. "Around that way, to the front, the door will be open." She lifted her chin to the left of the Wakefield House but would not take her eyes from the journal as she slowly turned, walking away toward her house.

"What if we get lost and can't find our way out? What do we do then?" I asked.

"Find a window to the outside and yell down. There are many along the way. But don't yell at night. I hate to be awakened."

Miss Flannery meandered farther away from us, and I looked up into the mass of beams and stones of the Wakefield House. Here and there were openings, surrounded by stone, and it gave me some comfort to know that, when we failed in our attempt to reach the top and had to come back down again, we could find one of these openings and scream for help. I looked at Thomas.

"You do realize you may never get the journal back," I said. "All that work and all those memories will be lost forever."

Thomas smiled and waved me on. "Come on, Roland. There's a great adventure to be had here today, and we're going to have it!"

It struck me then that Thomas understood something I didn't. The journal was a nice thing to look at, but everything in it was old and growing older. It was a record of our past, of things done before, of good and bad memories alike. Our journey was into the future and the adventure it held, and today that journey had led us to the foot of the Wakefield House.

This was one place where my character matched up with that of my brother. We were both fully alive at times such as these, when a seemingly impossible task lay before us and everything was at stake. I was more afraid and cautious than Thomas, but there was not an ounce less electric joy in my view of the circumstances.

The Wakefield House would be conquered or it would conquer us, and this was just the way we liked it.

CHAPTER 18

Through Haunted Passages

The Wakefield House rose so high into the air that it was easy to assume it wasn't very big around at the bottom. As we made our way to the other side, we were increasingly aware that this was a false notion. It was a six-sided structure, with sharp corners leading to each new side. The stones and beams looked more and more as though they'd been dropped out of the sky all at once and had only happened to fall in such a way that they all stood on top of one another. Colossal sharp rocks jutted out violently on every side and all the way up into the sky, with chunks and slabs of unfinished wood smashed in between. I was afraid to touch the Wakefield House, for fear that I might push it over and demolish the whole town in its crashing wake.

"There it is!" said Thomas, pointing down the side of the fourth outside wall we'd come around. He ran ahead, and when I came up beside him we both stood staring into a gaping hole big enough for a cart to fit through. There was no door, only the opening, which led directly to a set of stone stairs hidden in the shadows. The inside had a

169

quality I couldn't place at first. It was murky in there, and it smelled cold and alone. We stepped inside and walked seven or eight steps to the foot of the stairs, where it felt as if we'd arrived deep in the belly of the Wakefield House.

It was both quieter and louder. When we'd stepped inside, the Wakefield House wasn't creaking and there was no sound at all. Every noise from the outside world was gone. But when the Wakefield House swayed ever so slightly, the sound we'd heard outside became a roar of echoes. It began at the top — somewhere far over our heads — and descended toward us, moving through unseen halls and passageways, growing louder until the sound crashed into us at the bottom of the stairs like a screaming mouthful of hot air.

The coming fury of the sound reminded me of when Madame Vickers came swiftly up the hill on her horse and cart, clamoring violently toward her house. She would pass us on the hill very close, as if to scare us with the sound of hooves and rolling metal. My heart would race with visions of my fingers being crushed beneath the wheels of the cart, but then she would pass, and the sound would weaken, and I would listen until it died altogether at Madame Vickers's front door.

"This place feels haunted," I whispered, finally finding the right word to describe how the Wakefield House felt inside.

"That's exactly what I was going to say," said Thomas, who stood beside me craning his neck in every direction for a look around. It felt like a lot of lonely memories had been made here. If the walls could speak, I was sure they would bring a gathering gloom, a weight that could not be held up, like the very weight of the Wakefield House itself, and everything around us would come crashing down.

"Are we sure we want to do this?" Thomas said. I was surprised to hear him ask such a question, though his tone betrayed his motive. It was stated more as a taunt than a concern, and I thought the proper words out of his mouth given their meaning ought to have been, "You're not too afraid to go in, *are you*?"

Brothers often have a language all their own, propelled by a complicated mix of rivalry and love.

"There's a reason we're here," I stated flatly. "A reason not like all the rest who've tried. And besides, we've no place else to go."

Thomas looked at the rising stairs before us and clapped his hands together loudly, as if to shoo away all the bad feelings and prove that we were the only ones there, that there was nothing to be feared that lay sleeping and hidden in a corner. The sound of the clap echoed as I expected it would, but it died coldly and quickly as we marched toward the first of many steps we would encounter in the Wakefield House.

The pitch was far steeper than I'd imagined, more like a ladder than a set of stairs, and it went on far enough that we both had to rest before reaching the top. There was more light as we went, and as we came off of the last stair and onto the first landing there were two open windows, one on either side of us. We had entered a room that surprised and horrified us both. The surprising thing about the room was that we were suddenly in a place that was nothing like the outside of the Wakefield House. Gone were the sharp stones and clumps of wood clashing together unevenly, replaced by smooth stone walls and a perfectly even wooden floor. It was as if the builder had thrown the entire thing up solid – without an inside – then magically cut his way through, crafting it perfectly as he went. The center of the room was solid stone, and we had to walk around it to get a good look at both windows.

"This is amazing," I said.

"And worse than we could have imagined," added Thomas.

The horrifying thing about the room was the number of doorways. On either side of the two stone windowsills were eight openings, each one leading in a different direction along the outside of the room. We went all the way around the stone center and saw that some openings shot up on steep stairways while others headed back down. Still others turned sharply in one way or another. And there was something else, something worse still.

To the left or right of every single doorway, etched into the stone, were two harrowing words.

Wrong way.

It seemed as though different people had tried and failed at each door, found their way back, and left the little message to warn others, carving the words with a rock into the flat stone.

"But how can they all be the wrong way?" I asked. "That can't be right."

"Let's find out for ourselves," said Thomas. He walked through the nearest doorway, turning sharply to the right when he entered and moved out of sight.

"Thomas, wait!" I yelled. "The last thing we want to do is lose each other in here. We must stay close together."

We spent the next hour winding up and down passageways that turned nearly pitch-dark, then rose slowly with light as an approaching window came near. Every so often the Wakefield House began to roar from above, and we covered our ears until the frightening sound passed through. Sometimes we found ourselves higher off the ground, sometimes so low we could hardly believe it. And always we felt as though we were moving in circles, going nowhere at all. At length we looped back around to the room from which we'd begun, and we sat down beside one another exasperated, hungry, and tired.

"It would be good to have some of that yellow soup or some water," said Thomas. His voice was beginning to sound a little dry, and I cursed myself for not begging some water from Miss Flannery before entering the Wakefield House.

"The stairs that lead out are right there," I said, pointing to the way we'd come in. "We could sneak out, find some water and food, then try again."

"I don't think that's the way it works," said Thomas. "I have a feeling this is our one chance."

I had the same feeling, though I didn't say so.

"Should we try one of the other ways? The day is getting on, and this will be a lot harder without any light."

Thomas scratched his leg and looked thoughtfully at his knee, probably thinking the same thing I suddenly was. He rolled up his pant legs and revealed the marks across his skin in the soft light of the room.

"I wonder if these would be of any help," he said, though it sounded to me like he didn't really think they had anything to do with getting to the top of the Wakefield House.

I rolled up my own pant legs and sat staring at the markings.

"I've lived with them so long I think I have every line memorized," I reflected, running my finger along the pattern as I'd done a thousand times before. I had pulled my legs up toward my chest and so had Thomas, and just then I let my knee hang limp. It drifted toward Thomas's knee and rested there while I kept running my finger along the lines.

We sat like that for a long, quiet moment, and then Thomas moved his outside knee so that it was next to his other, the three knees — two of his and one of mine — sat together in a line. We'd never really thought to sit that way before and line things up, partly because there didn't seem to be any purpose in it, and partly because the markings on our knees were so different and we hadn't seen any real connection between the two. His markings were all of lines and squares, mine all of twists and circles.

"Come around the front," said Thomas. "There's something. . . ." He looked at our knees like he was looking at a message hidden under moving water, like there was meaning he couldn't quite see, though clearly *something* was there.

I shuffled on the floor until I sat facing him, and we knocked our knees together. I could only see my own knees clearly, the tips of where we touched like the peak of a small hill that drifted down the other side into Thomas's lap.

"Give me your hands," he said, holding his out in the air. We clutched each other by the wrists and pulled, lifting each other off the ground until we were even and could both look down on the four images coming together in the middle.

"Something's there," he said again. "Let's move to the window and try again."

It was rather dark where we sat, but when we moved under the light of the window and pulled each other up again, we both got a clear look at our four knees bunched together.

"Do you see it?" asked Thomas, excitement rising in his voice.

"I see it!" I exclaimed, and we both let go, tumbling backward and laughing out loud. We chattered nervously as we locked arms once more and held our position under the window. There, with our knees together, we saw the very room we were in. There were the eight doors and the two windows and, more important, there was a line that led a certain way, twisting and turning from my knees to his. My knees alone wouldn't show us how to navigate the Wakefield House, but our four knees together would.

"There are only a few hours of light remaining," said Thomas, glancing toward the window. "We'd better hurry if we don't want to spend the night in a haunted old house!"

"It begins with your knees," I said, looking intently at the fullness of the pattern. "With the squares and rectangles. But it ends with my knees, with the circles and swirls."

Thomas suddenly let go of my hands and I fell backward. He leaned forward, kneeling, then sat back on his feet. "This will be much easier," he said smiling, as if he'd figured out something rather obvious I should have noticed sooner.

I followed his lead and we touched knees again, this time with both of us kneeling on the floor. We were able to use our hands to point and decipher.

"The windows are here and here," said Thomas, putting one finger on each of his knees. "And this must be the stairway leading into the room." He pointed to a place where my knees met.

"That would mean," I said thoughtfully, pointing to one of the eight doors in the room, "we should go this way."

"That's right," Thomas said. "And that way is on my knee. All we need to do is follow it back and

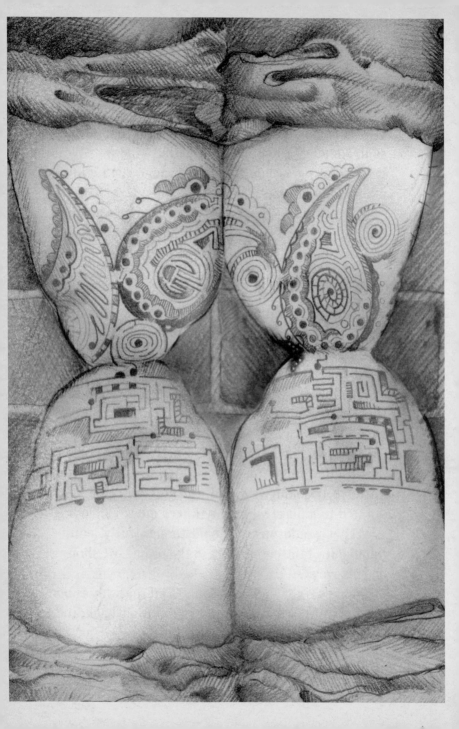

forth between my two knees until it crosses over to your side, here." Thomas pointed to a strange little symbol on my right knee. It was something I'd never understood, an image I'd looked at a thousand times.

The image gave me a chill, for it was clearly the beginning of a second way we must take, a way of swirls and circles that looked unbearably confusing. As if to provoke us into action, the Wakefield House began to groan from above.

"We'd best be on our way," I said, and we both hopped to our feet together.

We went through the door with Thomas leading, checking his knees whenever we came to a window where he could see clearly. We became lost only once during the next hour and then doubled back, finding our way again. The path never did lead back to the room where we'd begun, and it was very clear that we were rising steadily into the air. Each time we came to a new window we were another floor higher, until we were so high up it scared me to look out. The higher we rose the less noisy were the sounds the Wakefield House made, but the more noticeable were its sways. I truly felt that if I leaned out one of the high windows at the wrong time my weight would be enough to topple the Wakefield House on its side. Thomas had no such concern, and was quickly at every window we encountered, leaning out and looking up to see how far we'd come.

"We're almost there!" he shouted as we came upon a new room. The rooms were growing steadily smaller as we rose, and the one we were in wasn't much bigger than Madame Vickers's kitchen.

"Come look!" said Thomas, waving me close. I listened for the creaking sound of the Wakefield House. Then, hearing nothing, I walked to the windowsill, leaned out, and looked down. I could hardly believe how far we'd come. I could see Miss Flannery's house and even her horse. Both looked unimaginably small from such great heights. I turned my eyes to the sky and saw that we were only one floor from the very top.

"It sways a lot up here," I said, moving away from the window. "Do you think it will fall apart?"

Thomas knew I didn't like ledges and high places, so he also knew how to calm me down.

"It's been here a long time," he reassured me. "I think it can hold two skinny brothers just fine."

He looked at his knees, but only for a moment, and then he gazed at the two doors before us.

"That one," he announced with confidence. "The end is through that door."

We went out of the room, up a set of steep stairs, and then through a zigzagging passageway where it quickly became too dark to see.

"Do you know the way?" I asked Thomas, wanting to grab his hand in the darkness but finding myself too proud to do it.

"Just follow my voice," he said. "Skip the first opening you come to."

I did as I was instructed, feeling the open air of a passage we did not take. The way I was to go cut a sharp turn, and I bumped into my brother from behind.

"Watch where you're going!" he said.

"Very funny. Why aren't we moving?"

"Because we've come to the end."

I reached over my brother's shoulder and felt a wall of stone before us.

"We've gone the wrong way!" I said, suddenly losing my nerve and feeling claustrophobic in the black corner we'd wound our way into. "You must have made a mistake somewhere."

"There's no mistake," said Thomas. He was moving again, but I couldn't understand where he was going. I felt the cold of the walls with my hands and realized he was gone.

"Thomas! Where are you?" I yelled. A sliver of light appeared over my head, followed by the sound of something very old being opened and a flood of light pouring into the space where I stood.

"I'm here," said Thomas, looking down at me from above. With the light pouring in, I saw that there were notches in the wall for hands and feet and that Thomas had climbed up and pushed open a door. He climbed the rest of the way up, jumped inside the room above, and held his arm down to me.

"Come on!" he yelled down. "We've made it, Roland — we've made it to the top of the Wakefield House!"

I scampered up the stone ladder as fast as I could and bounded through the door into the soft light of a new room. As soon as I entered, Thomas let go of the door. It was heavy and only opened partway to begin with. It was restricted by a thick chain that would only allow it to open far enough for a person to get through. As soon as Thomas let it go, my heart sank, for when it closed it made a loud *click*.

"Thomas?" I said.

"What?" he answered. It was a voice mesmerized by what he had done.

"Was there a latch under there?" I asked.

"There was," he answered flatly.

We couldn't even see the door we'd come through, so perfect was its match into the floorboards of the room. There was no handle, no rope with which to pull the door back open.

The way from which we'd come was no longer open to us.

We were trapped at the top of the Wakefield House.

CHAPTER 19

The Circle of Light

The very top of the Wakefield House greeted us with a sway and a groan. The sound it made was almost as quiet as it had been when we were outside on the ground. There was only one window in the room at the very top, and the room was shaped unlike any of the rooms before it. All along the way as we'd come up it had felt as if we were near the outer edge of the Wakefield House, like there was a solid inner core that ran straight up through the middle, a core we were being kept away from on our ascent to the top. Some of the rooms we'd entered were on one side of the Wakefield House, while others were on the other side, and all the rooms were in some way curved like the middle part of a letter C. But this room was different, for it went all the way around in a circle, a thin passageway wrapped around a stone column.

Thomas and I walked around the passage, touching the column and moving toward the waning light of the window. The Wakefield House swayed so much at the very top it made me feel like I was standing on water with gigantic but peaceful rolling waves beneath me. When we came to the window we both looked out, standing next to each other, wondering why we'd been brought to such a strange place.

Far off in the distance — straight in front of our eyes — was the towering presence of Mount Laythen. We'd seen it off in the distance many times from the hill where we picked through garbage, and we were about as far away from it now as we had been then, only we were seeing it from an entirely different point of view. From the hill it had been cold and unknowable, but from here it seemed to invite us closer.

"Look." Thomas had pulled back from the window and was pointing to an oblong hole in the stone wall. It went deep into the thick stone to a shadowy place we couldn't see.

"Something's in there," Thomas continued, gesturing to the top of the rectangular opening where an image appeared. It was the very circle and square image we'd seen on the iron doors leading away from Mister Clawson, the same image we both had on our knees.

Thomas reached his hand inside, and when he pulled it out he had his fingers wrapped around something shiny with the gold and rubies look of a treasure.

"It's a spyglass," I said. "A very expensive-looking one."

Thomas extended the spyglass back and forth like a toy, laughing a little at how perfectly engineered it was.

"All this time, just sitting there, and it slides on golden rings as if it were only just made," Thomas commented. "Shall we have a look outside?"

It seemed like the obvious thing to do, and so with the sun hanging low in the sky, Thomas put the spyglass to his eye and stared out at Mount Laythen. He took his time, and I nearly crawled out of my skin with curiosity. Finally he took the spyglass from his eye and handed it to me.

"Somehow, I don't think you'll be surprised," he said, letting the spyglass go and stepping aside. And I *wasn't* surprised. There on the side of the mountain, in all its natural beauty, was the place where the image had first presented itself — the image on our knees, on the iron doors, on the way out of the Great Ravine. The image was there, a natural part of the mountain itself, exactly halfway up the side of Mount Laythen. A square and a circle, intertwined as one.

I looked at Thomas, who was smiling and jittery, clearly ready for what this meant.

"It's a long way off," I said. I was tired, thirsty,

hungry. I wasn't sure I was made of the same stuff Thomas was, and for a passing moment I felt I'd reached the end of what I could do. "I don't know if I can keep going."

This might have taken the wind out of some brothers, but it only made Thomas more animated.

"Think of it, Roland! Scaling the mighty mountain! It will be the time of our lives!"

He was pacing the floor, arms waving in excitement. "We've been *beneath* the world and *on* the world, but we've never gone *above* the world." He came to the window and looked out. "Not like *that*. It's where we were meant to go. That's the *right* place for us to end our journey. I can feel it, Roland. That's the end." He pointed hard toward Mount Laythen and looked at it with such affection I thought he might jump right out the window and try to fly there.

"There's only one problem," I said. "We're still trapped in the Wakefield House, and darkness is upon us."

The sun was halfway gone and fading fast, turning Mount Laythen into a black shape in the distance that looked less inviting by the minute.

It had been a remarkably long and challenging day, and it turned out that we were both a lot more exhausted than we'd imagined. For a short while we tried to look at my knees and figure out how to get down, but the constant swaying of the Wakefield House felt like a slow rocking chair lulling us to sleep. It wasn't very long before we gave up, lay down on the wood floor, and both fell into a deep slumber. When we awoke, light was pouring through the one window. We blinked and stretched and stood, trying to remember how we'd come to be in such a place, trying not to think about how hungry and thirsty we were.

"I wish I had my paint and paper," said Thomas, walking briskly around the circular stone center of the room and re-emerging at the window. He seemed to be trying to memorize what it looked like so that he might draw it or paint it later. He had a memory like that, a mind I could not understand. Looking at made things, he could see how they'd been built, imagine how he might build them himself, catalog the ideas for some later use I couldn't begin to imagine.

"We need to get out of here," I said, watching Thomas take the spyglass in his hand and gaze through it. "It might take a lot longer to leave the Wakefield House than it took to find our way to its top."

"You're right," he said, moving away from the window and placing the spyglass in his pocket. "Better have a look at those knees of yours again."

We spent a long time looking at the markings, trying to see how to get inside the center of the Wakefield House and make our way down, but there was nothing. The directions seemed to begin inside the center of the room, but there was no way to get inside the center of the room. It was solid, smooth stone and there were no doors or openings. We searched but could find no trick lever or knob that might unlock some hidden way through the stone.

"We'll have to think logically," said Thomas. "It's the only way."

Sometimes Thomas said ridiculous things like that to stop us from a downward spiraling frame of mind that he simply would not allow us to engage in.

"That's brilliant," I said. "Will we do it better if we stand on our heads, or should we jump out the window?"

Thomas laughed, but there was something about what I'd said that set him on a path.

"From the looks of your knees we are to start off from here by a new way, but we can't get into the new way because there's no door." He was rubbing his chin thoughtfully, and this time it was all comedy. He began to talk as though he were a very smart old teacher about to tell me a thing or two. "Now, Roland, if you can't get in by way of a door, what other way might you get in?"

I played along. "By way of a window."

"Exactly! By way of a window. There is only one way out of this room. The way we came in is closed to us now. The only way out is through that window." He looked suspiciously toward the opening where light poured in, and then we both went to the sill and stared out.

"We can't climb down the side of this thing," I said, leaning out and looking down at the crags and sharp edges of rock and plank.

"No, we can't," said Thomas. "But we could go up there."

He was craning his neck, looking up over the sill, and I joined him. There, just above the window, was a silver ring as big around as my neck. It was dangling from the wall at the end of a short chain that came to an end at a thick metal pin in the stone. Above it was another silver ring on a chain, and another. The rings stuck out from the Wakefield House and rose twenty feet above us to the very top.

"You can't be serious," I said, hoping desperately for another way. I looked up and down, seeing the harrowing distance to the bottom and the terrible climb that lay before us.

"Hold my legs," said Thomas. "I'll go up on the sill first, but when I do, you have to hold on to me. Hold on tight and don't let go!"

"Not a chance," I said, feeling a sudden urge to prove to my brother that I could overcome my fear of heights and make the climb. "I'll go. You hold *my* legs."

Before he could protest, I was up in the sill, crouching on the smooth stone. Thomas grabbed me around the middle of my legs and held tight as I rose up, leaning out of the sill and grabbing hold of the first silver ring. It felt solid as I yanked on the chain, so I slowly lifted my legs and gave it my full weight, hanging limp in the sill with Thomas's arms wrapped around my legs.

"Don't look down," said Thomas, loosening his grip. "You just *can't* look down, not ever."

My breath came in starts and stops as I lifted myself up and took hold of the second silver ring. When I reached for the third I was free of the windowsill, dangling a thousand feet off the ground in the open air. The rings were slick and my fingers were clammy, but I was a strong, wiry boy and I kept lunging for the silver rings until I had hold of the fifth one and I could put my foot into the first I'd left behind. After that, the going was easier. Step, grab, step, grab, until I was at the top, crawling over the edge, scared out of my wits.

"Here I come!" yelled Thomas. There was exuberance in his voice, as if he looked forward to

190

getting out on the side of the Wakefield House and showing me what he could do.

"Be careful!" I yelled back. "This isn't a game where you get two chances."

Thomas nodded and set his face in a serious look as he jumped into the sill and held on to the stone walls. He had no trouble getting the first silver ring into his hand and seemed to gain confidence when he reached out for the second.

"These things are slippery," he said, but he lunged for the third one nonetheless, and his feet were dangling free in the air. I almost couldn't bring myself to watch. If only he could get to where his feet could find a silver ring, the rest would be easy. But on the fourth ring his hand slipped and he shot out against the wall, swinging crazily from one hand.

"Thomas!" I screamed, reaching down in his direction and wishing he wasn't so far beneath me that I couldn't catch him and drag him to safety.

"I'm all right," he said, steadying himself, then grabbing for the silver ring with his free hand and moving once again. It was the only real scare of the climb between the two of us, and soon enough he was with me at the very top.

"You gave me a terrible shock back there," I said, my voice cracking and full of emotion. "Promise you won't ever do that again."

We looked at each other and a deep brotherly love passed between us.

"We're going to make it," Thomas said. "We're *always* going to make it."

I laughed and wiped my eyes, wanting only to get down to safety as quickly as we could.

"Let's get off this thing right now and never come back," I said, moving closer to the center of the top of the Wakefield House. It was flat and solid at the top, twenty feet across and littered with the past presence of birds that had made it their perch. Parts of nests lay scattered here and there, but we were utterly alone at the top of the world. In the very center of the top there was a large round opening, five feet across, and we crawled there on our hands and knees, the Wakefield House softly swaying beneath us as we went. When we reached the circle we lay down on our bellies and looked inside.

"This is the place," I said. "I wonder if anyone has ever come this far before."

"I think we're the first," said Thomas, a smile of excitement on his face. "Every step we take is one step closer to the bottom."

There was a chain hanging from the opening. Thomas reached down and grabbed it with both hands.

"Me first this time," he said. Before I could protest he was in the hole, holding the chain, shinnying fast to the floor beneath.

"Roland?" he yelled up. I could see him in the light, looking back up at me, dangling in the air from the chain. "There's a big room down here, but you'll have to swing away from the hole in the middle." He looked down and I could see the top of his head. "The hole looks like it goes on forever."

Thomas kicked at the edge of the five-foot wide hole he was hanging over and swung wide from side to side. Then he let go and the chain dangled clumsily below me. I followed Thomas's lead — climbing down, swinging wide of the hole, and letting go — and soon we were both standing in a well-lit room surrounded on all sides by jagged stone walls.

"It's not as pretty in here as the other rooms," I said, "And that hole must go all the way down the middle of the Wakefield House to the very bottom. It will light our way from the top, but it will get darker as we go."

The room had blown open at the bottom and was fifteen feet across. We stayed clear of the hole in the middle, and quickly saw that there were three winding stone stairways along the edge of the room. Each would lead somewhere different: one might come to a dead end; another might lead us in circles until we starved to death. We had not yet overcome the Wakefield House.

"Let's see those knees," said Thomas. We sat and looked long and hard before starting off. At first it was hard to tell which of the three descending stairs we should take, but soon the way became clear and we were off. Back and forth and down we went in wide and narrow circles. Sometimes we came close to the center and there were large openings where light poured through. There was a constant if very dim light throughout our bewildering circular voyage down the center of the Wakefield House. Many hours later — hours filled with checking my knees at light-filled holes in the walls, doubling back again and again, and stumbling over stones in the near darkness of some twisting portion of the way down — we stood at the very bottom of a perfectly round room.

"We've done it!" shouted Thomas. "We've actually found our way to the bottom."

There was only one dark passageway in the room, and it was directly across from the twisting stairs we'd come down. Between us and the opening to the passageway came the last of the light from the top of the Wakefield House. The hole in the ceiling where the light came through was smaller than the others had been. It looked like, if I could reach it, my head might fit through but not my shoulders. Beneath the tube of light sat a black stone pillar that rose to the height of my waist.

"What do you suppose that is?" asked Thomas.

"It's the last of the light," I answered. And it really did look like the last faint tube of light in the whole wide world, as if it were a candle and I could blow it out with a soft breath. We walked to the column together and stood over it, and Thomas leaned his head in to get a closer look. This cast a dark shadow over the top of the pillar, and I pulled him back by his shoulder.

"There's something written here," I said. "But we'll have to stay back or we won't be able to read it."

Thomas and I came around to the same side and moved in as close as we could, peering at the flat top of the black column. There was a smooth wooden slab on the top, and into it was carved an intricate message in the style of the images on our knees.

Listen, two sons of Warvold!
The end of your journey draws near.
Through two iron doors you have gone.
Through one more you must pass.
Open the third iron door and leave the
Wakefield House forever.
Its purpose is served. Its time has lapsed.

Look to the Dark Hills, where help may be found.
And here is something more to spur you on!
In the 6th Reign of Grindall came a man.
A man who rose up with force against an evil, and lost.
This man was your father.
You come now to finish what he began.

Sir Alistair Wakefield.

I read the last part twice before looking up, touching the carved word *father*, running my finger over the letters in the same way I'd moved my finger over the images on my knees for as long as I could remember.

"Can this really be true?" I stammered, glancing finally at Thomas beside me. He was uncharacteristically speechless, gazing at the message before him.

"I never thought of having a father before," he said after much thought. "I wonder if he was killed by this man Grindall. And what of our mother?"

The idea of having a father had stunned me, but something about the thought of a mother made me suddenly protective, as if I should rise up and find her – save her from whatever peril she'd gotten into. These were the kinds of thoughts — of a mother and a father — I had never allowed myself. They were pitiable ideas I had always feared would weaken me if I ever let them get a foothold.

"Are you ready to say good-bye to the Wakefield House and find the man who built it?" said Thomas. "Whoever Sir Alistair Wakefield is, we must find him. It appears he knows more about us than we know about ourselves."

We stepped away from the black pillar and moved to the opening of the passage. It would lead out of the heart of the Wakefield House, past the outer rooms, and directly to the last of the iron doors. There was no speaking between us as we went, only the sound of our breath and the shuffling of our feet. The passageway turned dark as we kept on, each of us with a hand on the wall to our side and a hand out in front in search of the door.

We found it at the same time, fumbling for a handle or a latch that would set us free.

"I've got something!" said Thomas. "Here." He took my hand and guided it to a handle big enough for us both to place a hand on. "Let's open it together and find Miss Flannery."

We turned the handle counterclockwise, and it clicked into place horizontal to the floor. Then we pulled, and the door groaned open slowly. Light poured heavy into the passageway, and to our great surprise the door teetered on its edge and fell back, the full weight of thick iron threatening to crash onto our feet. Thomas and I both jumped to the side as the door smashed down onto the stone floor of the Wakefield House.

"We've broken it," said Thomas. "Now the whole place will fall over."

He said this as a way to lighten the moment, and I laughed nervously at the idea of two young boys kicking the foundation out from underneath the Wakefield House so that the whole thing would tumble down in a pile of rubble. And then something not so funny began to happen: The opening where the iron door had been started to crumble. First there were only a few specks of dust in the air, but then a large stone fell to the floor in the opening, like a decayed tooth falling from the mouth of a monster.

I looked at Thomas, listening as the Wakefield House cried out with creaks and moans of stone against stone.

"Run!" we both screamed together, darting through the opening and out into the light of day. We kept running as we listened to the Wakefield House begin to crumble from the top. Looking back, I saw that it was leaning farther than it had before, whipping like a snake overhead, dropping rocks and beams from the sky.

"There!" yelled Thomas. He was pointing ahead, where Miss Flannery stood gaping at the falling building. We came alongside her, and the three of us watched the Wakefield House fall in on itself, then sway to one side and tumble to the ground in a twisting heap of wreckage. When the dust began to settle, I was surprised to see that it had fallen in a path that contained no houses or buildings. It had fallen backward, toward the Dark Hills. It seemed to point like an arrow in the direction we were to go.

"I guess we won't be seeing any more visitors," said Miss Flannery, surprisingly calm in the face of such a catastrophic event. People were gathering around the fallen tower, looking curiously at what had become of the Wakefield House.

Miss Flannery held her hands out.

"Here's your journal back," she said. "And your box of painting things. It's hard letting them go."

Thomas took the box of colors and brushes and the journal.

"I gather my protector has gone," mumbled Miss Flannery, "along with the profits of the Wakefield House." She turned to us, not coldly — but not friendly either. She seemed to want to send us on our way with a scare, a small repayment for what we'd done.

"Beware the coming fury!" she prophesied.

"Something watched over the Wakefield House, and that something will be looking for you."

I had the memory of a feeling then, of being watched in the mountains and the forest by something dangerous and unseen. I wanted to ask her what she meant.

"Can we at least have some soup?" asked Thomas. "There was no food or water in there." He pointed to the sky, where the fallen Wakefield House had been, then looked down at the sad remains. Miss Flannery stopped short without looking back. After a moment of quiet contemplation, we were invited once more into her home.

"I offer you water and soup, maybe a hunk of bread for your bag — but it must be quick. You don't want to enter the Dark Hills at night."

We followed behind her, the ruins of the once magnificent and strange Wakefield House behind us and a glorious bowl of yellow soup close at hand. But all my thoughts of the past and the future were dwarfed by the growing shadow of the Dark Hills and the unknown presence that awaited us there.

CHAPTER 20

THE WAY OF
YESTERDAY

"So you see," Roland told us, "we were two young boys then, a hard road behind us and what seemed an impossibly long way to go."

A soft breeze had invaded the dead air of night, and the *Warwick Beacon* rocked ever so slightly back and forth on the water. Neither Yipes nor I had said a word in the preceding hour, but it seemed that Roland had come to a place in his memory where he wanted to engage rather than merely tell. Yipes was accomplished at sniffing out such moments, and he leaped into the opening before I could even think to ask a question.

"How did you get the recipe from her?" he asked. "Did you steal it?"

He was speaking of the yellow soup, which we'd enjoyed many times on our voyage across the Lonely Sea. We'd asked Roland before how he made it taste so good and where he'd learned to make it, but he would never tell or let us watch him make it.

"All that's happened, and you want to know about the *soup*?" asked Roland.

"Yes," Yipes insisted. "I want to know about the soup. I love the soup! How did you get it?"

Roland looked at me in the moonlight, shaking his head in disbelief.

"Come on," Yipes prodded on. "How did you get Miss Flannery to give up the recipe?"

There were other, more pressing questions on my mind, but I said nothing. The banter between men amused me, and entertainment was hard to come by on the *Warwick Beacon*.

"If you must know," answered Roland, "Miss Flannery was very taken with Thomas's little paintings, especially the one of the Wakefield House from our approach to the Western Kingdom. She loved that painting. It reminded her of a time that had suddenly and irreversibly slipped away. Thomas offered to trade her for it. He was good at trading for things. By the time he'd finished bargaining with her, we had a jug of water, a loaf of bread, a collection of vegetables from her garden, *and* the recipe for the soup. All for the one painting, carefully torn from the journal and handed over."

"Astonishing!" said Yipes, and he truly *was* amazed, his mind wandering back to some distant memory of his old friend Thomas. "He had a way about him, a way in which he could get people to do as he pleased."

"I think if we'd have arrived in the Western Kingdom with a horse and cart we would have left there with arm-loads of treasure," said Roland. "Such were his skills of persuasion. The painting was a pearl of great price, at least for Miss Flannery — and Thomas was gifted at . . . shall we say, *developing* a person's needs."

"What did you find?" I blurted out, no longer able to contain my curiosity. "When you went into the Dark Hills, what did you find there?"

My own bleak memories of the Dark Hills had never left me. Hearing of them again had reminded me of the cold aloneness I'd felt amidst the sharp rocks and dry brush at my ankles on the long walk to Castalia.

"We come very near the end of my tale," said Roland, and I wondered if he was going to answer my question. "A good thing, too. We must get the both of you off to bed within the hour. Tomorrow brings work of another kind."

I wanted so badly to ask him what he'd alluded to from the beginning — what tomorrow would bring — but I knew his ways were mysterious and the answer would come in bits and pieces, not through direct questioning.

"Since you asked, Alexa," said Roland, "I will begin again an hour into our trek through the Dark Hills, when the thing we dreaded came upon us."

Yipes let slip a high-pitched, anxious laugh, trying to hide the fear he felt over what was to come and failing miserably.

"The feeling of being watched loomed over us," said Roland. "It was oppressive, like it would crush us both under the weight of its vigilant eyes. We were so very tired and miserable. You can't imagine the hopelessness of looking off in the distance and seeing Mount Laythen so far away. It would take days and days to walk that far, and we had every reason to believe we would never make it. Whatever it was that had been watching us all along was very near, and it seemed to me that it had stopped watching and begun hunting. I thought our first night in the Dark Hills was likely to be our last, and so it was."

"But you're alive, you're here with us," I said, uncharacteristically interrupting the captain of the ship. And then another thought occurred to me. "You must have been afraid."

"Only a fool or a madman would have been unafraid," said Roland. "I'm happy to say I'm neither of those things."

There was a brief pause as he came to the matter at hand.

"We had stopped for a drink of water, but there was no place to sit down. All the rocks were jagged and sharp, and the barren ground was cracked and hot from the scorching sun. We just stood there, trading drinks and gazing over the next ridge in the distance. At first I thought I was hallucinating — that it was a delusion formed in my weary imagination — but Thomas saw it, too. There, over the distant ridge, came the figure of a man. Only it wasn't a man. As he came into full view and bounded down the side of the desolate hill, we blinked our eyes and stared. What came for us was no man but a giant, and I tell you the truth, the ground shook as he came."

A smile crept onto my face but I didn't say anything.

"It can't be," said Yipes. "Can it?" He looked at me, puzzled but happy. We were both relieved as we turned our attention to Roland and saw there was a sly smile on his face. The powerful presence that followed Thomas and Roland had been someone we knew all along.

"Armon," I whispered on the wind. The Tenth City had swallowed him up and taken him away from us, but the sound of his name on my lips made my heart leap. He had been my friend and ally — the last of the mighty race of giants — and my mind drifted to a time when I rode high on his shoulders, Armon's long, black hair floating on the wind as he ran through the Dark Hills carrying me to some faraway adventure. The memory of him filled my mind as it always had, in such a way that nothing else fit, and I was overjoyed to hear him brought back to life in the telling of a story.

"We thought we might try to run away," said Roland. "But that thought quickly passed when we realized how fast he was coming at a walk. Had we chosen to run, Armon would have overtaken us without much effort. So we waited, shaking in our old, mismatched shoes and boots, assuming our lives were about to come to an end. As Armon came near, Thomas took out the spyglass — I don't know why — and held it. Armon bent down on one knee, his head still well above my own, and took the artifact in his huge hand, turning it round and round. He gave it back to Thomas, and then he spoke, and this is what he said:

"'Sir Alistair Wakefield will see the both of you. It's a long way — longer than you have in you — so you'll need my help.'

"He stood back up, towering over us, and stared off toward the Western Kingdom. 'I've been watching you awhile,' he said. 'I saw you enter the forest, the mountains, and go inside the Wakefield House. I have watched that house a long time, waiting for it to fall. My work there is finished.'

"That was all he said. Then he looked down at us both with a rather serious look on his face, as though he were sizing us up and trying to decide the best way to take us across the Dark Hills. He picked us up, and what transpired was one of the most astonishing nights of my life. It remains a powerful memory all these years later. Thomas in one arm and me in the other, carried over a bleak, moonlit terrain. There were times when I slept, bouncing as if I were seated on a huge horse, and other times when I was alert and watching the world go by. After a while there was some talking and we learned a little about him — nothing you don't already know — but he was coy when it came to Sir Alistair Wakefield. We knew only that the man was in some way connected to us, that he'd built the Wakefield House, and that he awaited our arrival.

"When morning broke on the Dark Hills we were passing through the Valley of Thorns, and Armon implored us to be very quiet. He had carried us through the night without complaint, though I had to wonder looking up how he might handle the mighty mountain yet to come. The Valley of Thorns was shrouded in a low mist, and we heard grunts and howls from somewhere in the distance. Armon moved like a great cat through the thorns, whispering to us not to touch them and to stay alert and still. Once we passed through, he went on until we stood at the bottom of Mount Laythen, where he set us on the ground and took a great jug of water from his back, drinking until I thought he would burst.

"'We've come to the way of yesterday,' he said at length. 'It's a hard way.'

"Looking up the mountain, I was struck by the thought that it was utterly impassable. The way was steep and violent, and Thomas asked if there were any other means of reaching Sir Alistair Wakefield.

"'There is, but this way is faster,' Armon told us. 'And more secret.'

"He had a contraption that held us on his back, for he would need his massive arms to navigate the dangerous terrain. He moved in such a way that it became clear he'd made the journey many times before, and soon we were high above the ground, bouncing precariously on the back of a giant on the way to meet Sir Alistair Wakefield."

Roland stopped and glanced over the water behind us. There were bits of cloth hanging from poles, and he watched them.

"The wind is picking up," he said, turning the wheel back and forth between his two hands and watching the

207

cloth strips dance in the air behind him. He took his pipe out of his pocket and began tamping tobacco into it.

"Why did Armon call it the way of yesterday?" I asked. There was a long, dreamy pause in which Roland lit his pipe and looked thoughtfully out to sea.

"Because it leads to the past."

And then he told us about finding Sir Alistair Wakefield in the secret realm beyond the way of yesterday, in the very heart of Mount Laythen.

CHAPTER 21

Sir Alistair Wakefield

There came a point when we reached the end of the very difficult climbing and Armon set Thomas and me down on the ground. There were blue and white patches of ice-encrusted snow scattered amidst the uneven rocks, and before us lay a path that went back and forth like crude stitching along a rising hemline.

"I believe I've carried you far enough," said Armon. He was, at last, showing a hint of weariness. I looked down the side of the mountain and off into the distance, seeing the Valley of Thorns like tiny pins far below and the wasteland of the Dark Hills beyond. Armon had carried us a long way in a short time, but it fell to me and Thomas now to finish the task.

"Let's keep going," said Thomas, already on the move up to the first switchback on the path. As we walked along, I passed a sheet of white snow and put the heel of my old black boot through the crusty ice covering. I reached down and dug into the hole I'd made and pulled out a fresh clump of snow, eating it as we kept on. It was the first time I could remember putting something so cold in my mouth. Chewing it up, I felt the sting of ice on my teeth and my tongue. I told Thomas he should try some, and we both ate snow and ice where we passed it here and there on the way up the path, looking back over our shoulders at the shrinking world below.

There had been a rising ledge as we went – the mountainside – but after a time we seemed to turn straight into the mountain itself, no longer switching back and forth along its edge. When the path turned once more, ice walls began to rise up on both sides. We were engulfed in what felt like a glowing tunnel of blue and green.

"We're close now," Armon said from behind us. I looked back and saw that he had to crouch down very low in order to make his way through. There was a chill in the air, and I could see my breath. Cold water was dripping everywhere and the ground was wet and slippery beneath my feet. Looking up, I saw a slick ceiling of clear icicles pointing down at me.

"It's growing lighter here," said Thomas, looking back from up ahead. He had turned a slight corner and I couldn't actually see him, but I hurried to catch up, watching my breath with some amusement. Soon I, too, noticed our way was filling with light.

"Roland, come quickly!" Thomas called. I broke into a slipping, sliding run until I came to a sharp turn and found my brother standing alone, looking down into a valley of green and blue and gold. Armon came up behind us licking a huge icicle he'd torn from the ceiling, and the three of us stayed there together, observing the world we'd crept up on. It was as if a giant bowl had been cut into the mountain, hidden on all sides by rock walls crawling with bright green moss, orange mushroom patches, leaves of yellow and gold. Near the bottom there were trees shooting up everywhere, and in the middle was a bright blue lake of cold mountain water.

"I know this place," whispered Thomas. And the way he said it sounded ghostly, as though he'd seen it in a dream and wasn't sure if it were safe or not. I felt something deep inside as well, some knowledge of the place before us, as though I'd lived an entire life here before but couldn't remember what I'd done. There was a boat sitting at the far edge of the lake, and this object in particular inspired something in my mind. I knew that boat, though I couldn't have said why.

"Armon, what is this place?" I asked. He was slurping the water off the icicle, and with his free hand he pointed down and to the left, near the line of trees that edged up against the blue lake. There

211

was a home, or a building of sorts – I couldn't decide which. It was tucked in tightly to the trees as if it were hiding there.

Armon tossed the icicle aside and it broke into a thousand pieces. "Down we go. The rest of the way is easy."

And it *was* easy, a winding path through trees that wasn't too cold and wasn't too hot. The sound of birds was everywhere, and they flew from tree to tree in a jumble of noise as we went. There were small animals darting up the sides of trees – squirrels of a sort I'd never seen before. They were entirely gray or black, and they looked at us curiously as we came down into the realm of Sir Alistair Wakefield.

"He won't be like anyone you've met before," Armon said as we approached the blue lake and walked along its wide belly.

"How do you mean?" asked Thomas, pulling his paints from his pocket and stopping to make a picture. I think he was a little nervous to go on and was looking for an excuse to stop.

Armon didn't answer Thomas, but he didn't seem to mind that my brother had stopped to paint a picture. It rather seemed the most natural thing in the world to rest a moment, breathing the sharp, cool air, watching the rings from the feeding fish blip on the surface of the water. I glanced at the page Thomas was painting and saw that he'd gone back in his memory and was drawing the cave of ice and the view from above. He drew them both at once on two adjoining pages, moving back and forth between the images as he changed colors, swishing his brush in the water of the lake. The lake was so blue I half expected the wet brush to come out the same color, and everything Thomas painted to come out infused with sapphire.

"We should be going," said Armon after a short time. "We don't want to keep the old man waiting too long." It was our first clue as to what we should expect: He would be old. This pleased me, for I had a certain sense that someone old would be gentle with age, would be kinder than someone young. Thomas put away his things and we walked on.

Soon we came to the thing we'd seen from above, and looking straight ahead we saw that it wasn't a house at all. It was a vast wooden terrace, held above the ground on a complicated system of fallen trees. It was leaning wildly in different directions, as though it might fall over in ten ways all at once, and somehow this very fact made it stand up and seem indestructible. And what was more, the terrace went back into the standing trees behind it in a way that looked untamed. It rose and fell, higher and lower in the trees, and there were rooms up there — small houses, if you will — wrapped around the larger trees at odd intervals along the way.

"It's a little like the Wakefield House," I said. "Like it should fall to pieces, but it doesn't."

"It looks familiar, don't you think?" said Thomas. I didn't think so — not really — but it did have a certain power over me, like it was drawing me to it. There wasn't very much time to wonder about the sprawling wooden structure before us, because right after Thomas asked his question, someone came out onto the high terrace and looked down at us.

"I was beginning to wonder if you'd gotten lost." It was a man, leaning over the railing from above. His voice was gravelly but clear, and it was filled with a sense of loneliness being drawn away, like he'd been by himself a long while and suddenly everything about him had changed with our arrival. It wasn't the words he said, but the way he said them that betrayed his happiness at our arrival.

"These boys have grown," said Armon. "They're not as easy to carry as they once were."

What did he mean? Had he carried us before? The time to ask about such things seemed wrong, and I held my tongue.

"Grindall will be looking for me," Armon

continued. "Better I return home and put aside any suspicions."

"Stay for something to eat, then go," said the man on the terrace. Then, looking at us, he added, "Bring me the boys, won't you?"

Off to one side there were stumps of trees that served as a stairway, rising higher as they went with nothing to hold on to. Armon was first to go and we followed, hopping through the air from one stump to another until we were even with the terrace above. When we reached the top I was concerned the structure wouldn't hold Armon's full weight, and to my further alarm he didn't step onto the terrace, he leaped onto it, as if he were actually trying to crash into it and knock it down. But the terrace didn't so much as sway under the monstrous pressure of our giant friend.

"The Wakefield House hasn't fared as well," said Armon as Thomas and I stepped onto the long, open landing ourselves. "It's lucky there were no houses in its path."

"How I would have loved to see it tumble over!" said the man with a longing sort of smile. He looked at Thomas and asked, "Did it fall over just when you two opened the iron door?"

"Almost," answered Thomas. "It swayed a little at first — so we could get out of the way — and then it fell over."

While Thomas talked, I observed the man on the terrace. He wasn't as old as I thought he would be – maybe fifty. He had a physical strength about him that made me wonder if he could wrestle Armon to the ground. It wasn't that he was big – rather he was solid, like a rock, like you could drop a house on him and he would walk away unbroken.

"I planned it that way, so that once the deed was done, the Wakefield House would stand no more," said the man. "And it would only fall the one way, the way in which Miss Flannery was not to allow anything to be built."

"Are you Sir Alistair Wakefield?" I asked, my voice shakier than I'd expected it to be.

He looked upon my brother and me, nodding, smiling a happy smile. "I am he."

Thomas started to open his mouth, undoubtedly to ask the first of many questions, but Sir Alistair Wakefield silenced him with a raised finger.

"First we must eat and get Armon on his way," he said, and with that he turned from us and walked along the wooden terrace into the thick of the trees. Thomas and I followed with Armon close behind us, crouching under branches as we went.

"You will enjoy this," said Armon, laughing just a little. "He has a way of welcoming visitors that you won't soon forget."

We went along, rising and falling on the wooden path beneath us, looking out over the rail to the ground below until we came to an egg-shaped platform with one large tree shooting up the middle. There at the base of the tree waited Sir Alistair Wakefield, and around him was a feast like nothing I'd imagined in my past at the House on the Hill. There were platters of cooked fish, breads with sweet spreads of honey and jam, pitchers of things to drink, and cheese with crusts of colors I'd never seen before.

"It's all been sitting here a little longer than I'd planned," said Sir Alistair, sitting down among the bowls and plates. "But I think it will be all right."

We sat together under the big tree – eating and drinking – and very quickly we came to call Sir Alistair Wakefield simply Alistair, for he insisted on ridding our first meeting of formality. Soon we began to ask him questions, and he, being a kind man and wanting to enlighten us, was happy to sit beneath the tree for hours and hours and tell us all we wanted to know.

❧ CHAPTER 22 ❧

THE STORY OF OUR BEGINNING

Roland pulled his logbook out of his pocket and looked at it thoughtfully as midnight approached. We had brought more candles onto the deck of the *Warwick Beacon* and lit them, so that it felt like a small cathedral on the rolling sea. I couldn't remember the last time I'd sat silently listening for so long, the rising and falling of quiet water trying but failing to lull me to sleep.

"And here we come to the whole of the matter," said Roland, "the unraveling of the past. This part of my story is best told as a tale within a tale, unhindered by the fullness of a hundred questions from two brothers on that cool, crisp day on Sir Alistair Wakefield's terrace."

"A tale within a tale," said Yipes. "That sounds good to me."

Roland glanced once more at the logbook in his hand and seemed to grip it more firmly. There was a hesitant look about him for an instant, and then he held the logbook out to me over the pale light of candles, as if he wanted me to take it from him. Yipes lunged for it, wanting to see the ever-secret logbook for himself and overcome with a desire to have it. But I was quick when I needed to be, and I

218

snatched the secret treasure from Roland's fingers and clutched it to my chest. I expected Yipes might wrestle me onto the deck for it, and I envisioned the two of us rolling around under the sails, battling over the prized logbook we'd never been allowed to see inside of. But Yipes only sat wide-eyed, staring at me, his breathing a little heavier than it had been.

"You may open it," said Roland, a twitch of excitement in his sandpapery old voice.

Feeling a little sorry for Yipes but still uncertain whether he might try to take it from me, I held the logbook out in the open air above the candles, gripping it tightly. Yipes moved close to me where he could see, and we both read the words on the cover.

Into the Mist

The words were burned into the old leather, but they were black and clear as day. *Into the Mist.*

"Why, it's Thomas's journal!" exclaimed Yipes. "You've had it all this time and have never shown it to us?"

Yipes was reaching for it, trying to pry it open or out of my hands, so I clutched it once more to my chest. This was a treasure beyond all imagination, a connection to Thomas Warvold that would help me understand him, that would draw me nearer to him. Part of me was angry Roland hadn't given it to me sooner, knowing what he knew about my link to his brother Thomas. I didn't want to look just yet; I wanted to savor each page, to slowly touch each of the paintings Thomas Warvold had made.

"You'll find I've scratched a few notes in there along the margins, but not many," said Roland. "Mostly I just look at the pictures. But I've looked at them long enough.

"If you want to know what Alistair told us that day on Mount Laythen," he said, "all the facts are written down in the back of that book. Since the book is now in your possession, maybe you could read it to us and give an old man a moment to gather his thoughts of what remains."

I lifted *Into the Mist* from my chest and quietly turned to the back, flipping rapidly and glancing away as my finger fanned the edge of each painted page. Yipes leaned in close and kept putting his hand out in the fanning pages, trying to stop them from turning so fast, but each time he did, I moved the journal away where his short arms couldn't reach. I wanted an hour or a day with each page; I wanted to imprint each image in my mind, to savor the book. I arrived at the very last few pages and, from the corner of my eye, could see that there were only words and tiny sketches, as if Thomas had taken a moment here and there in the telling to scribble in the margins. I cleared my throat and held my hands a little closer to the candlelight. Then I read what was written in the back of the book, and it began with a single name on a line all its own.

Grindall.

Grindall.

To know your past you must hear this name, for it is he who set you on the way to yesterday, into the secret realm of Mount Laythen. He ruled Castalia, the land your father lived in. His descendants rule it still.

Grindall was a cruel man. Through cunning and deceit he attained supremacy over the race of giants and used them to force his will on the people of Castalia. He used trickery to achieve his throne, and violence to keep his power. He did not love the people he reigned over, and this turned his heart small and black over time.

But your father was not the kind of man who scared easily, and he was compelled to lead a secret rebellion intent on removing Grindall and the giants from power. There were three years of quiet planning in dark corners of dark rooms, gathering weapons and plotting every detail. It was during these three years that the two of you were born.

When you, Thomas, were three, and you, Roland, were two, revolution came to Castalia. Your father led every detail of the uprising. He was at once a man of great courage and astounding intellect, a leader of the kind from which legends are made. But there are times in which a legend is made not on the battlefield, but in the desperate hour of defeat. And so it was with your father.

221

He failed in his attempt to seize the throne, though he very nearly succeeded. There came a moment in the conflict in which your mother and the two of you, though hidden well, were discovered by the enemy and taken to the Dark Tower. It was said that you — his only children — would be spared if only your father would lay down his sword and end the uprising.

And it was here — in the hour of defeat — that your father changed the course of history. I am very sorry to say that your father and mother were not spared, but were made to climb to the very top of the Dark Tower and walk a narrow plank until, together, they slipped and fell into the open air. All of Castalia stood below and watched them descend, but all turned away as they reached the bottom. All but one.

You sit now in the presence of that one, the giant Armon, for he is the one giant who has always secretly been the enemy of Grindall. In the end it is he who has made all the difference.

With the death of your father, the rebellion was put down. Grindall had learned an important lesson: There would be others who might try to rise up against him, but they could be stopped before their time, if only he knew who they were. From then on, every Castalian boy and girl was brought before Grindall in the Dark Tower at the age of five and again at the age of seven. Grindall eyed them carefully, gave them sweets, asked them questions. He was looking for certain traits — boys or girls who had it in them to become leaders of some distant rebellion. If they were unusually smart, he kept them. If they were rude and boisterous, he kept them. If the other children seemed to follow them about, he kept them. These children were never returned, and they became known as the lost children, gone forever.

But even Grindall had his limitations for doing evil, and it fell to Armon to get rid of the lost children. It was Armon's responsibility — his sworn duty to Grindall — to do away with all of them. Grindall chose them, but he sent them immediately to the underground realm of Armon, in the dark beating heart of the tower.

You were the first, the two of you. The first lost children. And you were by far the youngest — at only two and three — to ever have such a heartbreaking name. Before any of the other lost children knew their fate, you were already gone! Seeing your father and mother destroyed by Grindall had made Armon think dangerous thoughts. How could he get rid of two boys, and yet not do away with them? There was one place that struck him — one place where two small children might not be found.

By cover of night, Armon took you out past the great lake, to a secret place known only to a few. He took you up Mount Laythen — by the way of yesterday — to the very place you find yourselves in now.

"How many lost children are there?" asked Yipes. "How many have there been?" He was very curious about children being taken from their parents and hidden away.

Roland didn't seem to know or didn't want to tell. He only said there were many, and that as far as he was aware, all of them had been saved by Armon.

"How long did this go on?" I asked, adding the years up in my mind and coming to a bigger number than I thought possible.

"Through all of the last five reigns of the line of Grindall, to the very days leading up to your own encounter with the last of them."

"*Victor Grindall,*" whispered Yipes. "The worst of them all."

"Not true," said Roland. "All the others were as bad or worse. Victor Grindall was a madman, and that set him apart from his ancestors, but those that came before him were as cruel as he was. They wanted only to have power, as much as could be had, and it was the power itself that eventually did them in."

I thought about this idea for a moment in the quiet of the night, listening to the ancient wooden boards of the *Warwick Beacon* creaking on the soft waves. *A quest for power ends in despair. There is no other way.*

"Shall I go on?" said Roland. "And tell you about our time with Sir Alistair Wakefield? There are things we learned there that I think you'll find interesting."

Yipes and I both nodded vigorously, and I clutched the

precious logbook to my chest. I felt I hadn't really paid for it with something of my own, and there was only one thing I possessed that seemed a worthy gift in return.

"Roland," I said, pulling something from my own pocket, something I'd carried with me all the way back in the days of walled cities and visits to Bridewell. "I want you to have this."

I held my mother's spyglass out over the candles. She had etched and painted it so perfectly, with all the colors and paisley patterns I loved to look at, but I knew then that it hadn't always looked that way.

"This is the spyglass you retrieved from the Wakefield House, isn't it?" I asked.

Roland looked longingly at it, as though he were back in the twisting halls with his older brother, trying to find his way out. "It is the very same one."

"Did Thomas Warvold give it to my mother?" I asked.

"He did," Roland answered, taking it carefully from my hand. "And now it comes full circle, back into my possession. It's no small thing, you giving me this."

I had the feeling then that he'd always wanted it back but hadn't been able to ask me for it. It was hard to let it go, because it was something that took me dancing into the past whenever I held it or looked through it. I always expected to see something exciting when I put it to my eye, and this was a feeling I'd come to long for.

Roland put the spyglass in his pocket, and in a way it

was gone forever. He would let me use it, but it would never be truly mine again. Looking at the logbook in my hand, I knew Roland felt just as I did. We'd both lost something, and had both gained something.

"Off we go then," said Roland, suddenly full of vigor. "I don't mind telling you, my memories of our time with Sir Alistair Wakefield are among my favorites. And we must finish within the hour if you two are to get any sleep at all tonight."

He began again, taking us back to a time and a place of deep magic I hadn't anticipated.

CHAPTER 23

The Past and the Future

At some point between all the questions and the eating of too much good food, I became exhausted in that special way in which a great task is complete and rest comes naturally. All my senses started to shut down at once as late afternoon crept over the terrace. It felt as if the tremendous strain of the previous days had caught up to me all at once.

I slept for a few hours, then woke briefly as night was coming on, and I saw Thomas lying next to me. Armon was gone.

"He'll be back soon enough," said Alistair, who sat close by rocking in an old chair he'd brought out from somewhere. "Go back to sleep. You need rest more than anything."

And so it was that we slept through the night, awakening in the morning to the sharp smells of ripe berries and the wonderful aroma of fresh baked bread floating over the terrace. For some reason my mind drifted away from the lost children and the story we'd been told of our past. The idea of my parents falling to their deaths hung over me, but I must say it was like a distant haze, as though time were drawing the memory out on a piece of thread and I could only grasp at it. I realize this sounds strange, but we were drawn into Alistair's world in a way that made time seem less meaningful.

"You come now to a time of training and of reawakening your past," said Alistair. We did not fully appreciate what this meant the first time we heard it, but within a few days under the guiding hand of Sir Alistair Wakefield, it became very clear what he'd meant. In the morning hours he focused all of his considerable knowledge directly on the two of us, as though he'd been awaiting our arrival for a long time and had planned out an entire curriculum for us to learn. There was a brief time of learning together, and then he would single one of us out while the other tinkered on some project he'd assigned.

To Thomas fell the vast storehouse of Alistair's architectural genius. He taught Thomas how to build all kinds of things, beginning with small scale models of the terrace and the Wakefield House. I was astounded to find that Thomas seemed to already have the knowledge stored somewhere inside him, and that Alistair was only awakening it with the lessons he taught. Such was Thomas's extraordinarily rapid mastery of complicated subjects. Soon they were talking of vast walls miles and miles long, of catapults and towers, of all sorts of things I found no interest in whatsoever.

My lack of interest might have been a problem had this been a school we were attending, where building unimaginably complicated structures and objects was the only thing to learn. I believe I would have been removed from such a school and regarded by everyone as a student of catastrophically limited ability. Thankfully, Alistair seemed fully aware of my limitations from the start, and in fact had not the slightest problem with it. If anything, it pleased him, for his plans for my education were as different from those he had for Thomas as one could possibly imagine.

On that very first day – and every day after in our time with Alistair – he spoke to me almost exclusively of the ways of water. My time was divided between the lake and a certain room on the terrace. The room was hard to find at first, and I often became lost looking for it. The terrace wound through the trees in such a confusing way that I never felt as though I could know all the places it went. I always used the tree in the middle – where we'd eaten on the first day – as my point of reference. But I still became lost now and then and had to slowly wind my way toward the water until I knew again where I was. The room had a sign over the door that read THE WARWICK ROOM, and the inside was filled with things I came to love. There were piles and piles of charts and diagrams of places I'd never seen, all of them on the water. There were complicated plans for a boat much larger than the one in the lake, and there were books with instructions on sailing and nautical science. I devoured everything I saw, spending hours poring over the books, the charts, and the plans.

While I was busy learning the ways of water, Thomas was spending most of his time in the modeling room. From the moment he laid eyes on the modeling room, it was his favorite place in the entire world. It was here that he and Alistair built scale versions of all sorts of things. There was a complete model of The Land of Elyon with every imaginable detail. The two of them would explore every nook and cranny, speaking of how the land might change, where new things could be built, and what places could be explored. They used every kind of tool one could imagine — saws and clamps, boxes and devices, measuring instruments, brushes, glues, paints, and papers of all kinds and sizes. It was a treasure trove of creative implements, and the mere thought of going there set Thomas to smiling and dreaming of what he might build next.

And there was something more, something that is harder to describe, though I will venture an attempt. There came a moment in our training when I was sitting with Thomas alone. We had long since been given a room of our own, wrapped around a tree like all the others, with desks and beds and a window that looked toward the lake. Alistair was preparing lunch, and we'd come back between lessons to get what we needed for the afternoon activities.

"Thomas," I said on this particular day, "how long do you suppose we've been here?"

Thomas began to answer right away, but then he stopped himself, scratching at his chin as he sometimes did when he was feeling particularly puzzled over a problem in the modeling room.

"Why, I guess I don't know," he said. "I've lost track of things with all the work."

"Do you remember when Armon brought us here? Can you remember when that was?" I asked. It was very odd, but neither of us could remember. It seemed to us both that he'd been gone only a few days, and yet it felt like we hadn't seen him in years and years.

"We could ask Alistair," said Thomas.

"Ask me what?" Alistair had come to the open door of our room and was standing there looking at us both. I suddenly got the same feeling about him as I'd had about the time passing. Maybe it was because my mind was on the idea of time — I don't know. But all at once, Alistair looked like he was very, very old . . . and yet very, very young. Everything about that moment hung in a disorienting timelessness. I sat down on my bed, dizzy from the swirling thoughts in my head, and I looked once more at our teacher.

"What is it, Roland?" he asked. "Is something wrong?"

"How old are you?" I replied, and for some reason I felt ashamed of asking, like I'd uncovered some secret I wasn't supposed to. Alistair backed up a step or two — I remember that — and he had a look on his face I understood. *I hoped I wouldn't have to explain this just yet.*

"The both of you, come with me," he said, looking at us not with anger but with resolve — the time for telling something important had come, and he was bound and determined to tell it. He took us to the best part of the terrace, a place where I could see the lake and the boat, the rising trees, and the colors of the canyon walls. There were three chairs — ones we sat in all the time. This time when we sat, Alistair took a deep breath.

"We've been busy, haven't we?" he started. "It's easy to lose track of time when you're so busy with so many important things."

He seemed a little confused, trying to find a

way into what he wanted to say, and so Thomas helped him along.

"How long has it been since Armon left us here?" my brother asked. "For some reason we can't seem to remember."

"That's a complicated question," said Alistair, "though it may sound simple when you ask it."

Alistair scratched the hair on his chest through his shirt. The hair had always struck me as one of the old parts of him, all gray and fluffy at the edge of his collar.

"I don't know," he finally continued. He had a bewildered look on his face as he repeated himself. "I don't know how long Armon's been gone."

"Well, what about a guess?" Thomas prodded. "How long would you guess?"

"I have no idea," said Alistair. "Maybe ten days, maybe ten years. There's really no way of telling."

"But that makes no sense," I said with uneasy laughter. "You have to know *about* how long he's been gone. Don't you keep track of the days or the weeks? It can't be that hard. And we *can't* have been here ten years."

"Can't you have?" said Alistair, and this time he was serious, as if he wanted to make sure I knew he really thought it was possible. "Maybe you just don't remember."

233

I asked Thomas later if he'd felt the same way I did at that moment, and he said that he had. We both felt suddenly old. Questions ran through our minds: How was it that Thomas could be so skilled as an artist at such a young age? How could two boys — ten and eleven years old — unravel the mysteries of the Lake of Fire and the Wakefield House?

"This place you've come to, it's ancient," said Alistair. "It's the *first* place, and it has a certain problem understanding time."

"How old are you?" asked Thomas, and the moment he asked it I knew the answer wouldn't make any sense.

"I'm two hundred years old," said Alistair. "At least that's what Armon tells me."

"But that's not possible!" My words came out louder than I'd expected them to.

Alistair scratched once more at the gray hair under his shirt and stood up out of his chair, holding on to the rail of the terrace.

"We come now to the whole truth," he half mumbled before continuing with a question. "Do you remember what I told you about Grindall, about the giants?"

Thomas and I both nodded.

"A long time ago, I lived in a place Grindall passed through, a place that has since been left

234

behind. They call it the City of Dogs now, though it wasn't always so. I built much of what used to be there. In fact, that is the place where I built the first thing I was ever really proud of: a clock tower. It was the center of everything then, the place where everyone gathered. I built the first boats that sailed on the great lake at Castalia; I built so many things. It was a gift I had — building things. It came naturally to me.

"The very first Grindall came through there, and I saw him standing before the clock tower. He was just an average man then — or so it seemed — peddling potions and remedies that quickly got him run out of town. Something told me I should keep my eye on him, that I should follow him. It wasn't until much later that I realized the inkling I had to follow was the hand of Elyon."

"The hand of Elyon," repeated Thomas in a whisper, as if it meant something he'd felt himself at times.

"I followed Grindall out into the wild," continued Alistair, "and found that he'd come into our small town not to sell us something, but to see if we were organized and well armed. He had the race of giants with him, of which there were about a hundred, and he was making his way to someplace only the giants knew of."

Alistair stopped short and offered to bring us the things he'd set out for lunch, but we insisted he go on without delay.

"He was possessed, you see," said Alistair. "By an evil force that knew the way. . . ."

"Knew the way to what?" I asked.

Alistair hesitated, looking back over the years in his mind. "The way *here*. The way to this sacred, hidden place, where all language is the same, and where time stands still.

"I followed Grindall and the giants, and when they departed with a bag full of Jocasta stones, I remained. There have been times when I've gone away — to build the Wakefield House, to . . ."

He broke off, as if there was something he'd stepped into and wished he could turn back.

"Where else?" asked Thomas. "Where else have you gone?"

There was a long silence, during which I had the feeling again of time passing and yet standing still. Did the moment last a second or an hour? I couldn't say for sure.

"Do you see that boat there, on the lake?" asked Alistair.

We told him that we did.

"There's a bigger one, at the bottom of the cliffs, on the Lonely Sea."

236

"You mean below the clouds?" I said, my mind racing with the thought of it.

Alistair nodded. "The *Warwick Beacon*. I built it a long time ago, long before your father rose up against Grindall, before there were any lost children. Back then — when it was only me — I had years and years to work. Through six reigns of Grindall men I was mostly alone — alone but for one."

"Armon," I said. "Armon came to see you."

"He did. It was his might that made the *Warwick Beacon* possible. He was often tasked with searching The Land of Elyon for what he might find for Grindall, and so he would sneak back, though none of the other giants ever did. Each time he returned, he would tell me he was sorry it had been so long, and I would say back to him that it hadn't seemed long at all. But years had been passing without my knowledge."

"But why didn't Armon grow old as well?" I asked. "He should have died out in the world, away from the power this place has over time."

"If you were from around these parts — from Castalia or the City of Dogs — you would know that giants don't age in the same way humans do. They can be killed, but they grow old ever so slowly.

"I came here before the first Grindall overtook

237

Castalia. Your father rose up in the sixth reign of Grindall, a hundred years later. I was here that entire time, and yet I was not."

"Tell us where you went, Alistair," I pleaded.

"There were many years away, building the Wakefield House, followed by many years building the *Warwick Beacon*. And then there were journeys to the Great Ravine and the Lake of Fire."

He saw that we were surprised he'd been to these places of our past.

"Oh, yes, I know all about those places. I had a little something to do with the iron doors, the signs and symbols along the way . . ."

He trailed off again, deep in thought.

"That time away aged me, but there was something else that aged me even more."

"What? What else took you away from this place?" asked Thomas. We were both terribly curious.

"The Lonely Sea," answered Alistair. "Time on the *Warwick Beacon* aged me a great deal."

"You've sailed the Lonely Sea?" I asked. Something about the thought of it thrilled me. I'd been sailing in the lake with the small boat for — how long? — I didn't know. But the idea of taking a bigger boat on bigger water to unfound places filled me with excitement.

"You must believe what I'm about to tell you," said Alistair, a desperate tone in his voice that I had never heard him use before. "I have known many daunting tasks in my life — the construction of the Wakefield House and the *Warwick Beacon*, immeasurable travels by land, sailing the Lonely Sea alone. In all these things I was led by an unseen hand. I've often thought I was a lunatic — a madman following dreams and feelings that seemed to have no purpose. But there came a time when everything I'd done made sense — the day Armon came not alone, but with the two of you strapped to his back."

CHAPTER 24

The Five Stone Pillars

We could get no more out of Alistair, and he wandered off to retrieve our lunch. While we ate, we pestered him with questions, but he sat quietly, unwilling to add to what he'd already told us.

The day was drifting by. It was strange to think that night would come, followed by a new morning, and yet I would not have aged. I would be the same. It struck me that I could be a child forever in this place, that I would never grow old or grow up. There was something altogether wrong about the idea of it, and I tried to put it out of my mind.

After a while we were finished with our lunch, and Alistair told us to prepare for a long day of walking in the mountains.

"When morning comes, I'll take you both to the *Warwick Beacon*," he said. "It requires all of a day to get there, and Armon will be coming again soon. When you've been here as long as I have, you get a feeling about such things, and I sense him coming. He won't be alone."

Thomas and I glanced at each other and knew

what Alistair meant. We would soon share Alistair's affections with an unknown number of lost children.

I couldn't get to sleep that night, and neither could Thomas. He sat at our little window with a blanket wrapped around himself as he painted pictures by candlelight. He seemed to be going through more pages than I'd seen him use up before, as if he were trying to empty his memory of images he'd seen along our way so that he could fill it back up again. I watched him at the window for an hour or more, and then I forget what happened, so I must have fallen asleep. I awoke early to find him snoring beneath the window, clutching the book in one hand and a brush in the other.

"Thomas," I said, kneeling down beside him, "it's morning. How long did you stay awake?"

He came slowly to life and stretched his arms over his head. "Too long." He said this at the tail end of a yawn and it came out garbled. "But time stands still here, remember? So I might have slept an hour or a year. Who's to say?"

It was a good point, though it confused me. I was finding time to be a topic that could drive me crazy if I thought about it too much, going round and round in circles and never reaching the end. I was quickly getting in the habit of thinking about something else when it came up, which I imagined was how Alistair came to have no idea how long he'd been alive. He'd probably resolved not to think about time anymore after a hundred years. It had taken me only a few days.

There came a knock at the opening to our room.

"Are you ready to leave?"

It was Alistair, a very large pack I'd never seen before over his shoulder and a jug of water on a sling in his hand. He held out the water.

"Thomas, would you mind carrying this? We'll need it for the first few hours. After that there are waterfalls and streams we can drink from."

Thomas untangled himself from the blanket and took the jug of water. The three of us started off, out of our room to the end of the terrace.

"That's a very big pack you have there," I said. "What's inside?"

Alistair didn't answer me as we made our way down the stump stairs to the ground below. He said nothing as we rounded the lake and ventured into the trees on the other side. Somewhere along the way I sensed an odd feeling and realized it was only odd because I hadn't felt it in a long while.

"I'm a little tired," I said. "Can we stop a moment and have some of that water?"

Alistair took in a deep breath of mountain air

242

and released it. "We've come away from home. It feels good to be getting old again."

That must have been it. Time had moved back in. I was growing up once more, and though I was tired, I was glad of the change. After some water, we kept on, and soon enough we were on the other side of Mount Laythen, looking down on the cliffs and the cloud-covered sea. Both were nestled closer than I'd expected.

"Alistair," I said, feeling that we'd come far enough without questions to try once more, "how many lost children has Armon brought to you?"

"Seventy-one," Alistair said without the slightest hesitation. "Usually in groups of three or four, though he once carried six up the way of yesterday. I don't know how he managed it. Though I suppose it's just the sort of thing a giant would try to do."

There was a pause as he shifted the mighty load on his back, then he went on.

"They never aged, never grew up. It was good they didn't have to stay too long."

"Where have they all gone to?" asked Thomas, picking up my line of questioning as we came to a narrow, trickling stream that crossed our path. We leaned down for a drink, cupping ice-cold water in our hands.

"Somewhere safe," said Alistair. That was all he would tell us — there was no more — but I got the

243

feeling we were going to find out soon where this safe place was.

Hours later, when we'd finally wound our way to the bottom of Mount Laythen and walked to the cliff's edge, it was late afternoon and we were all tired, but we didn't stop to rest. Alistair slipped the huge pack off his back and dropped it on the ground with a dusty thud. He breathed a sigh of relief, then surveyed the edge of the cliff, searching for something.

"There it is," he said, gazing a few feet off to one side. There was an iron ring sticking out of the rocks. A thick rope was attached to it.

"Can the two of you pick up that load and bring it over there?" He pointed to the iron ring, walking toward it. Thomas and I each stood on either side of the pack and found cloth handles to grab hold of it. We lifted together and discovered the load was unbelievably heavy. Alistair was even stronger than we'd imagined.

"What do you think he put in here?" I whispered. "A stack of rocks?"

"Or maybe some of Armon's old boots," Thomas ventured.

I laughed and grunted picking up my side, and straining, the two of us hauled the pack over to where Alistair stood. He was pulling the rope up, winding it carefully in loops at his feet. When we arrived beside him, I saw that it was more than just a rope — it was a rope ladder to the *Warwick Beacon* below. When Alistair had the rope ladder all the way up, it was carefully stacked in a tall pile beside him. At the very end there were loops and extra lengths of rope, which Alistair tied to the pack. When he was satisfied the load would not come loose, he asked us to push it over the edge. He held the rope ladder firm and we did as we were told. Then Alistair slowly let the rope ladder all the way out again.

"The pack will help keep it steady from the bottom as we go," he said. Then he pointed to me. "You first, Roland. It will be a little disorienting getting through the clouds, but after that it's easy. You'll be fine."

My heart raced at the thought of climbing down the side of the cliff, but not for the reason one might think. I wasn't afraid. I was overcome with the thought of standing on the *Warwick Beacon* and of sailing the Lonely Sea. I raced to the rope ladder and started down — faster than I should have — and Alistair scolded me from above.

"Slow down, Roland! The *Warwick Beacon* isn't going anywhere!"

I paced myself then, taking each step carefully until I was surrounded by clouds. The rope ladder was a little moist, but it became dry again once I made it through. I stopped in midair and looked down . . . and there it was! The *Warwick Beacon* sat bobbing on the water. It was the first time I'd ever seen it, and it was without hesitation the most magical moment of my life. Looking out over the Lonely Sea for the first time and seeing that boat, I knew my destiny lay on the water.

The farther I went down the rope, the more I found myself in open air. The cliffs, it seemed, did not go straight up, but rather pointed in like the right side of a V. The pack sat on the deck of the anchored *Warwick Beacon* as though someone had carefully set it there. Touching my foot on the wooden planks of the deck filled me with a sudden, consuming emotion. *I've found my home at last.* It was all I could think of. In many ways the first leg of my journey ended in that moment, on the deck of the *Warwick Beacon*, gazing out onto the vast Lonely Sea.

"What do you think of her?" said Alistair. Both he and Thomas had come on board while I was lost in my own world.

"She's perfect," I answered. "And so is that." I pointed off the side to the endless water before me. When I looked back, both Alistair and Thomas were smiling, but they were sad smiles, as though they knew something heartbreaking in that moment that I hadn't yet come to realize.

"Take a good look at the cliffs," said Alistair. "You won't be seeing land for a while."

"How long?" asked Thomas. "I have projects half finished back home. When will I get back to them?"

It was the first time I'd heard the slightest bit of animosity in his voice, as if my training were taking precedence over his own.

"We'll be gone about thirty days," said Alistair. It was a shockingly large span of time, and came as a surprise even to me. Thirty days at sea? It was unimaginable for Thomas.

"But that's too long!" he shouted. "I'd rather be left behind than be gone from my own things for weeks and weeks."

He looked back at the rope ladder, still attached to the pack.

"Don't you want to know where your brother is going?" asked Alistair.

Thomas looked back from the rope and his eyes passed over Alistair to me. There was a lost hope in his expression, but he seemed to accept the idea of a long time on the water. He nodded, smiled awkwardly, and asked just the right sort of question.

"Can you show me how to sail this thing?"

And then I smiled too, very happy to have such a good brother. "I can show you," I said. "It's not as hard as putting together a wall or a building like you're used to. This will seem easy."

Alistair had given me untold hours of instruction on the lake in what I now realized was a miniature version of the *Warwick Beacon*. The boat on the lake was much the same, only it had been a third the size. Thinking back on it now, I felt like I'd had years and years of instruction in the skills of sailing, reading maps and compasses, and studying weather. Maybe I had. It was so hard to tell how long we'd been with Alistair. As the sails rose and filled with air, I felt a surge of energy in my chest and cried out, "Whooohoooooo!!"

"You take the wheel," Alistair told me. "Thomas and I will unpack everything I hauled over here. There's already a lot stored belowdecks — water and dry goods — but the bag has more things we'll need. Head directly north, and don't bother to call for me unless you're in a real jam. I feel the rare and wonderful opportunity of a nap coming on."

"Where are we going?" I asked, taking hold of the wheel, feeling the wind-worn knobs of wood in my hands.

"It would be foolish to think ours the only world," said Alistair. "Elyon is much bigger than that!"

And so it was that we sailed across the Lonely

Sea for many days and were told a great deal more about our lives. We learned that we'd stayed a while longer than we might have imagined at Alistair's home when we'd first been brought there at the ages of two and three. Indeed, we'd stayed a good long time — seven years — before he took us to the orphanage in Ainsworth. He'd taken me on the boat on the lake countless times in that seven years, shown Thomas how to draw little pictures and build with blocks. But in the end he knew that we couldn't stay two and three forever. We had to grow up, and that could only happen somewhere far away from Grindall, where we could not be found.

He'd already set about creating the Wakefield House and placing the iron doors in our path before we arrived — all guided by what he continually called "the unseen hand of Elyon." It was a dangerous way, set out but not chosen by Alistair, and I felt a great satisfaction in knowing the challenges had been so big and we'd overcome them all.

There was only the matter of the markings on our knees to lead us back home when the time was right. He had, in fact, planned to make our way a little more direct, but found that once again he was compelled to set our course and let nature do the rest. He had wanted to come get us or to send a sign, but something had compelled him against it.

And so he looked — day after day — in the direction of the Wakefield House, wondering if it would ever fall over and our presence would be known.

He surmised that our path was one set out by hands not our own, and that there must have been some learning we'd needed in the journey itself. He told us over and over to remember every detail of how we came to be in his home on Mount Laythen, to search for those things that seemed to be put there for our knowledge and benefit.

We also learned that Alistair had taken this journey at sea before — many times, in fact. After Grindall and the giants left him, Alistair's first task had been to build the terraced home he lived in. Shortly after its completion he was at work on the *Warwick Beacon* (with the occasional help of Armon), and soon after that he began sailing it in search of a secret place. It took many years to build the boat and more years still to search the Lonely Sea, and all the while he was away from his home, getting older.

There had been an image in his mind that haunted him — an image of looking up at five pillars of stone shooting high and thin and jagged out of the Lonely Sea. At the top the pillars gently mushroomed out, but he couldn't say what might be at the top. He had attached a name to the vision in his mind — *The Five Stone Pillars*.

On the morning of our fourteenth day at sea, Thomas and I awoke to find Alistair at the wheel. The wind had picked up in the night and drawn us quickly to the east. The fact that I knew this upon waking was unusual, but I simply knew it was so. It was as if I had a compass and a map inside me, so I could feel where I'd been and where I was going. I looked at Thomas rubbing the sleep out of his eyes and reaching immediately for his book and paint box, and I wondered if it was the sort of feeling he got when he was painting a picture or building something. Those sorts of things had always come hard to me — like they were a foreign language — but the language of the sea was not like that. It was my language. And in this way I learned to appreciate my gift and the gifts of others. I stopped coveting the unattainable talents Alistair and Thomas enjoyed, and started embracing my own way.

"Thank you for coming along," I said to Thomas. "I know you didn't want to."

We both stood and started for the wheel where Alistair waited.

"You seem happy here, on the water," my brother observed as we walked the wooden planks of the *Warwick Beacon*. "It makes me think our paths might not always be the same."

I felt a terrible, deep sadness when he said that. It had never occurred to me that we might not always be together, that a fork might come in our shared path where he could walk away from me. It was the sort of thought I was in the habit of dwelling on, and I was thankful to come alongside Alistair and have him change the subject.

"There," he said firmly, pointing straight off the front of the *Warwick Beacon*.

Before us lay miles of rolling blue water, but way off in the distance, almost beyond our sight, something had appeared. I knew what it was before Alistair named it, and my heart leaped at the idea of having found this secret place in the vast openness of the Lonely Sea.

"The Five Stone Pillars," said Alistair. His gaze turned squarely on me, and he waited until I took my eyes off the five black pillars in the distance and looked at him instead. He bent down on one knee and put his hand on my shoulder.

"Do you know how to get here?" he asked.

I looked at the Five Stone Pillars, then out to sea in another direction, then back at Alistair. It was a funny thing, but I absolutely *did* know how to find the Five Stone Pillars. I nodded slowly. Then Alistair stood and guided me by the shoulder to the wheel of the *Warwick Beacon*.

"This ship is yours now, Roland. I'm growing too old for adventures such as these."

I put my hands on the wheel, shaking with fear

and excitement at the thought of having the *Warwick Beacon* for my own. And then Alistair said something almost as surprising as his offer of the ship.

"You'll soon come by this way again, but we're close enough for today. It's time you took us back home."

CHAPTER 25

In the Shadow of a Giant

There were a few times — when I got very tired — that I relinquished the wheel of the *Warwick Beacon* to Alistair on the way back to Mount Laythen, but I did most of the sailing and all of the navigating. It took seventeen days to find our way back over the Lonely Sea, plus another day to make our way up and around the mountain to the home of Sir Alistair Wakefield. The last bit of evening light sparkled on the lake as we finally arrived at the foot of the terrace. We were still on the ground — about to start up the stairway of tree stumps — when a voice came from above.

"I was starting to wonder if you'd ever come back."

It was the unmistakable voice of Armon. He came slowly into view, leaning his huge shoulders and head over the terrace into the twilight. "Where have you three been hiding?"

"Alone, are we?" Alistair skipped the usual pleasantries of welcoming an old friend.

"They've gone to sleep," said Armon. "Three of them — two boys and a girl."

"How long have you been here?" asked Alistair. The three of us were making our way up the stairs now while Armon moved around on the terrace to keep us in view.

"Five days, I think. You know how this place is. It's hard to know for sure after a day or two."

We reached the top of the stairs, and Alistair nodded with some concern.

"And how long were you gone this time before you returned?"

"That I can tell you without worry of getting it wrong," answered Armon. "I've been away a little over two years."

I looked at Thomas and saw that his head was swimming just as mine was. We'd been living with Alistair for *two years*. It didn't seem possible at first, but thinking over all I'd learned and done, it seemed almost not long enough.

"Where were you?" asked Armon. Alistair moved over to the table by the terrace where we always sat together and everyone followed. It was a relief to slump into one of the chairs and look across at the shadowy mountain. The sun was down and little light remained.

"Showing them the Five Stone Pillars," said Alistair. He looked at me with great pride and something else — some sort of deep longing. "We have ourselves a new captain, as I'd hoped."

Armon set his gaze on me from above, pretending to look me over with some concern as to whether or not I was fit for the task.

"I suppose you'll do," he said at length, but it was clear to everyone he was very pleased. Then he added, "You'll have more trouble keeping the children under control than making the trip. They're *spirited*, if you get my meaning."

Thomas, who had been quiet until then, broke in.

"Alistair, how many will fit on the *Warwick Beacon*?"

Alistair scratched the white hair on his forearm and considered the question. He had settled into his chair and had the look of someone content with his surroundings.

"I've never taken more than six at once, but I suppose it could hold a dozen or more if the need arose."

"Why do you want to know?" Armon asked, bending down on one knee and staring at my brother. "You've got something on your mind. I can tell such things."

I knew what Thomas was thinking, that keeping a promise he'd made was important to him.

"Would you be willing to make a slight detour on your way back to Castalia?" Thomas asked, returning Armon's gaze. "I think Roland will want to come — so you might have to carry us both awhile."

"Where is it you'd like to go?" asked Armon.

Thomas looked at Alistair briefly, then set his eyes on me. "Madame Vickers's House on the Hill."

There were some very brief introductions the next morning in which Thomas, Alistair, and I became acquainted with the three lost children. They were — as Armon had said — spirited. I was dumbfounded by the endless number of questions they posed — *When can we see our parents? Can we play in the lake? What's this?* and *Can I have that?* and on and on and on. Then the three of them would go running off down the terrace chasing one another or playing at hide-and-seek.

"You must be gentle with them," Alistair said to me. "Endure their questions. You can give them a future at the Five Stone Pillars — a good home — but it won't include their parents, and this will hurt them."

And I was, from then on, always kind and gentle with the lost children. They were prone to crying at night and getting into mischief during the day, but these are stories for another time, for on the first night after our return from the sea, Armon took Thomas and me to a place from our past where we had a duty to fulfill.

We spent a good deal of the journey from Mount Laythen to Madame Vickers's House on the Hill telling Armon about the owner of the home, her son Finch, his two dogs, the wretched conditions, and all we'd had to endure. Armon, being a virtuous creature, walked through the night with great speed — such was his enthusiasm to come face-to-face with this terrible woman and her loathsome son. It was just breaking dawn when we arrived, the three of us walking side by side with Armon in the middle. We crept up the side of the hill until the house was in view, and then we told Armon to remain hidden until we called for him. Both Thomas and I had a flair for the dramatic, and we weren't going to miss our chance to make the most of our circumstances.

We strode up the hill to the house and soon heard Max and the Mooch barking, which had the effect one might suppose: Everyone was quickly awakened. The first to show his face was Finch, who came bounding onto the front porch of the old house with a large wooden club in his hand. The first light of day seemed to stun him and set him back on his heels a little, and he put his arm up over his face with his free hand.

"Who's there?" he shouted, blinking furiously

as he dropped his arm and spotted the two of us standing in the dirt. Children started flooding out the door past Finch. All the girls and boys who lived on the hill were soon on the porch, pointing and cheering and yelling our names. There were new children I didn't recognize and others who'd grown a little older in our absence. And something I wouldn't have expected had taken place while we were gone. Our leaving had become a thing of legend and late-night whispers, our return awaited and long hoped for. They'd taken Thomas at his word and *expected* us to come back for them — it was only a matter of when. All of the children began streaming down the steps and onto the hill. Soon they were dancing around us, yelling out questions and greetings.

"Get back in the basement! All of you!" screamed Finch. He was waving the club over his head when suddenly Madame Vickers appeared behind him, pushed him out of the way, and stood motionless, her hands on her hips. I wouldn't mention it were it not such a sight, but to see her in the morning was something to behold. Her hair stood like a wild cone of lightning on top of her head, and her face was pinched in a profoundly mean expression, as though waking her from sleep was an offense punishable by the most painful kind of torture. From within that horridly pinched expression arose two bulging, angry eyeballs that seemed altogether too big for the face to which they were attached. Oddly, she'd either taken the time to put her boots on before coming out onto the porch, or she'd never taken them off when going to bed the night before. Either way, she stood before us in a rage, a nightshirt dancing at her knees, the ghastly boots in full view rising up her shins.

"You children get in the basement this instant, or there will be no breakfast!" She was cold and calculated in her words, and the group that had formed around us lost its nerve and began to disperse in her direction.

"We promised we would come back for you if we could," said Thomas. He had his eyes trained firmly on Jonezy, the new boy that had arrived at the House on the Hill on the very day we'd left. He was older now — everyone was — and it was strange to think that we hadn't aged so much as they had in our absence.

"No breakfast!" howled Madame Vickers. She walked three steps forward to the edge of the porch and Finch came up next to her, smiling and tapping the wooden club into the palm of his hand. She leaned out over the steps of the porch and screamed, "Get back to the basement!"

"NO!" yelled Thomas. The defiance and courage in Thomas's voice set Madame Vickers back for an instant, but then she turned to Finch, tore the club from his hand, and marched down the steps toward us in those awful boots that were made for kicking.

"Thomas," I said, "maybe now would be the right time to call Armon. She's *really* angry."

The crowd of youngsters scattered in every direction and Finch ran around the side of the house yelling over his shoulder that he was going to get the dogs. I was beginning to wonder if Thomas had gone frozen at the sight of those black boots and that dreadful face about to descend on him. And then he said that magical word, and the scene before me was transformed.

"Armon!"

He yelled it not with dignity and grace, but more like a war cry, like the cry of a young man about to charge into battle and carry the day. It was magnificent!

"What are you babbling about now, boy?" said Madame Vickers. She stood over Thomas and reached the club over her head, ready to strike my brother to the ground. Max and the Mooch were rounding the corner with Finch close behind; he was laughing wickedly at the idea of so much violence about to occur.

A shadow came over Madame Vickers's face, and I was reminded once more just how big Armon was. He was coming up the hill behind us, his huge strides pounding the garbage on the path into oblivion, and he had come into full view. There wasn't a closed mouth among us – everyone stared, slack-jawed and mystified by the coming fury of such a magnificent being. All at once he had his arm out over our heads and took the club from Madame Vickers's bony fingers. She released it without complaint, and Armon pushed me and Thomas gently aside.

It is very hard to describe how someone so mean – someone who had held such power over us – could fall so far so fast. Madame Vickers was so small and frail standing in the shadow of Armon, I felt truly sorry for her in that brief moment before he spoke. Max and the Mooch had run back behind the house, but Finch remained, backpedaling toward the porch.

"You," said Armon. His voice was not loud, but *big* like a mountain. He was pointing at Finch. "Come stand here by your mother."

I had a feeling then that Finch couldn't do it, that he would run away and hide, and so I felt I should try to help, if only a very little. "He won't hurt you," I advised, "if you do as he says. But Finch – you can't escape him. He'll find you."

Finch blubbered as he came, and I don't think to this day I've ever seen anyone quite so afraid. It took a while, but finally he arrived beside Madame Vickers, wiping his nose with his shirtsleeve, unable to look up.

"No more children for you," said Armon, and Madame Vickers jumped as though Armon had clapped his hands in front of her face. The power of his voice was almost more than she could bear. There was a fierce wind in it, as though he was very angry and could barely contain himself. He clenched his huge fists, and they made a grinding, popping sound.

"We'll take all the children," he went on. "And this place will be no more."

Armon put one huge hand on Madame Vickers's shoulder and the other on Finch's. Then he commanded them both to look at him. "I'll be back this way again," he warned. "You would do well not to attempt to fool me."

And then he released them. The moment he did, Madame Vickers and Finch ran off, hitched up the one horse and cart, and rode off down the hill of garbage with Max and the Mooch yelping and running behind.

"We found a better place for you," Thomas told the other boys and girls. "I've seen it with my own eyes." The crowd was in something of a state of shock, unsure what to think of Armon and all that had just occurred. But then Armon got down on his knees and smiled at the group of eleven lost children standing amidst the garbage.

"Thomas is right," said Armon. "There's a better place for you — a place you can call home, where no one will take advantage of you again."

They still seemed afraid and wouldn't come near him, so I walked right up to Armon and punched him as hard as I could in the knee. Armon knew just what to do, for he had been winning over lost children of a different sort for a very long time. He toppled over as if my little fist had been too much for him, and as he lay on the ground I dug through his pockets and found a brightly colored candy.

"What do we have here?" I said sternly, unwrapping the treat and popping it in my mouth.

The children shuffled forward slowly, and then Armon put a candy in his own mouth and smiled so big and so silly and made the most outrageous *mmmmmmmmm* sound you can imagine. The children came to him then — they ran to him, dove at him, tackled him, rolling around in the dirt trying to get the candy from his pockets and all the while he smiled and hummed *mmmmmmmmmmmmmmm*.

Thomas and I stood there laughing, and then we looked back over our shoulders, watching the dusty trail of Madame Vickers's cart snake its way toward Ainsworth.

"She's gone," said Thomas. "She's really gone."

A cheer rose up around the House on the Hill, and we looked back to find Armon's hand open, all the brightly colored candies being taken by smaller hands and popped into eager mouths.

Soon our group was on its way, walking toward Mount Laythen . . . and a future in which my days of wandering the wide world with my brother were about to come to an end.

CHAPTER 26

A Fork in the Wood

I'll never forget the day of our arrival with the eleven children from the House on the Hill. They were older than the children from Castalia by four or five years each, and every one of the boys and girls from the House on the Hill took at once to playing big brother or big sister to the younger children on the terrace. It was a day of watching them explore the wonders of Sir Alistair Wakefield's home, with me and Thomas remembering what it was like when we'd first arrived there. The group of fourteen was always together after that — no matter when I saw them — and it seemed to me that they had been marked for one another from the start.

"It's time I was on my way."

These words were spoken by Armon the very next day, and it was the beginning of a series of good-byes that would last until my heart was nearly torn into pieces. When he'd left the first time, I'd had this wonderful feeling that I would see him again. That sort of feeling has joy in it, because longing for something tells your heart that it will one day come to pass, either in this life or the next. But when Armon said those words — *It's time I was on my way* — there was a finality in them that broke something deep inside me. And I think there was something else — something even deeper — as if I'd only just begun to feel a new and terrible emotion in the wake of Armon's leaving.

I remember embracing him and having my feet leave the wooden floor of the terrace as he lifted me into the air. I could get my arms around his neck just enough to lock my hands together, and I did this, hoping he would never make me let go. I remember sobbing in such a sad way that my body shook against his chest and I wouldn't look at him or anyone else. I loved Armon then for a special reason only a brother can know. I knew what was soon to come — I could feel it in my bones — and this moment with Armon let me pour out all my loss and fear at once, to release it into his care, to let it go and move on.

Not long after he was gone — maybe a day or two or three — Alistair pulled me aside and we walked along the blue water of the lake together. Thomas was busy at building things once more, and already he was in the habit of spending entire days in the model room.

"There are times in a young man's life when two paths appear before him," said Alistair. His hands were locked behind his back as he walked, and there was a melancholy smile on his face. "That time has come for you, Roland, and it must be faced."

There were tears welling up in my eyes, but I fought them back and looked off toward the lake. Alistair stopped and put his hands on my shoulders. He wouldn't go on until I looked him in the eye.

"I have a deep feeling of a coming catastrophe," he said. "Grindall's war machine grows more frightening, or so Armon says. A man such as Grindall won't stay put forever."

He looked down at his feet, then back at me. "Neither of you can stay here as the world around you grows darker. You must each play your part as we come to a fork in the path."

We walked on quietly, and somewhere along the edge of the blue lake Alistair whispered, *"Path leads to path."*

In everything he'd said before, there had been a glimmer of hope that I might yet find my way back to the people and life I'd known, but in those four words my sadness deepened. *Path leads to path.* It suddenly seemed possible that the whole of my coming adventure would be had on paths of water, while Thomas's would be made entirely of land.

"It's time I grew old, don't you think?" said Alistair.

"You *are* old," I said, and this made him laugh a little.

"I think you know what I mean," he said.

"Where will you go?"

"I was hoping I could go along with you – to the Five Stone Pillars – and I could spend the rest of my days as a grandfather of lost children."

I thought this sounded like a very good idea.

"Besides," he continued, "you'll need to know how to bring the *Warwick Beacon* in close to the Five Stone Pillars. It's . . . *complicated*."

I didn't ask then what he meant, but I thought a great deal in the days that followed about what sort of challenges awaited me at the bottom of the black stone columns that rose from the Lonely Sea.

"We leave tomorrow morning," Alistair said as we turned and headed back in the direction of the terrace. "Best we finish packing and say a difficult good-bye."

I busied myself with preparations, doling out responsibilities to the boys and girls who would soon be leaving the home of Sir Alistair Wakefield. There was electricity in the air as we talked of the journey ahead and the place we were going. The looks on the faces of the fourteen boys and girls made me very happy for them. I knew how they felt, at the start of some grand adventure, and a part of me longed to be on our way. I didn't see Thomas at all as he busied himself in the model room. I think we were both afraid of what might happen if we encountered each other so close and yet so far from my departure. We were not sentimental with each other, and the thought of it confused us both. It seemed best to go about our business until the very end.

Late that night I went to our room and found it empty. I sat on my bed and looked across the room we'd shared, and then I lay down facing the wall. I was just nodding off to sleep when Thomas crept in quietly and got into his bed.

"Good night, Roland," he said softly.

"Good night," I replied.

And that was all we could think to say before drifting off to sleep.

There was a lot of activity the next morning as we readied the group and the supplies for what would be a special two-day trip with small children to the *Warwick Beacon*. I kept trying to find a moment of peace in which to pull Thomas aside, but each time our eyes met from across the terrace it seemed that either he or I was being pulled in some direction. Maybe we were happy of the distractions — able to put off the inevitable good-bye for just a little longer – but there was a part of me that began to regret not having spent more time talking with my brother in the days leading up to our parting.

There came a time when all was prepared and everyone was ready to leave, and it felt to me as if the moment arrived suddenly and without warning. Everyone lined up and took their turn saying good-bye to Thomas. When it came down to only me and Alistair remaining, Alistair seized the moment and went straight up to Thomas, hugging him as a father might do when he knows he'll be gone a long time. There were words between them, but they were secret words that were not meant for my ears. I heard only what Alistair said at the very end, and it seemed as though it was said for my benefit as well as Thomas's:

"Don't stay on here too long."

When Alistair turned to go, there was a determination in him, as though he knew it would take all the strength he could imagine in himself to actually leave this place.

"Come along then," he said, waving everyone down the stairs, each with some small or large supply to carry. "Let's give two brothers a moment of peace."

I have a memory of being in the Ainsworth orphanage as a small boy and playing out in the dirt in the courtyard with all the other children.

And there was this one time when I was digging a hole, and I could hear the bell go off and the sounds of children yelling and playing as they filed through the big door that led inside. I remember looking up and hearing the silence of the moment. Only a second ago there had been a clamor of noise and activity, and then there was nothing, only me and the haunting stillness. It felt that way now. There had been so much separating my brother and me – all the bodies and sounds and tasks – and suddenly there was nothing between us but a lingering stillness.

"I don't know if I can do this," I said. And I really didn't know. Thomas had always been there. It had been his strength that carried me beyond the House on the Hill, through the Lake of Fire, out of the Wakefield House – and so much more. I didn't know if I could navigate the Lonely Sea without him. More important, I didn't want to.

"Take this with you," said Thomas, coming toward me. He was holding out his book of paintings.

"I can't take that from you," I protested, finally unable to contain my emotion. "Your whole life is in that book."

"*Our* lives are in there," he corrected. "We're always together if we can look at our past. But we can't *live* in our past, Roland. We have to go on."

272

"But if I take the book, you won't have it," I said. And then finally I told him what was truly in my heart. "You won't remember me."

Thomas smiled the way he always did when he'd pulled one over on someone. It was never a smile that said, *You see there! I got you!* — but a smile that told how much he liked you, how much he enjoyed being with you. He reached behind his back and into a pocket, and pulled out a second book that looked about the same size as the one in his other hand.

"You don't always have to make models in the model room," he said. "It's a good place to paint as well."

He handed me his original book, and I began to flip through its worn pages. He followed along, turning as I did, and I saw that he'd painted the book all over again. Though the new paintings were a little less smudged or torn, it was hard to tell the pictures apart.

"You did this for me?" I asked.

"I did it for us, so we would always remember. I don't want you forgetting me, either."

There was no embarrassment or awkwardness then, only brotherly love as we embraced on Sir Alistair Wakefield's terrace.

"How long will you stay here?" I asked as we stood apart again.

"Not very long, I don't think," Thomas answered. "I want to go back to Ainsworth, to the old orphanage. Something tells me I should make an appearance there, throw my knapsack over my shoulder, and wander out of town. I want to go see Thorn and take a look around the woods and the mountains. I have a feeling I'll be building something near there someday."

It all sounded very adventurous to me. And dusty. And unlike anything I really had much interest in doing.

"I believe I'll be on my way," I said. Then, looking at the book he'd given me, I added, "I won't forget you."

"I won't forget you, either."

Thomas stayed and watched me go down the stairway of stumps. When I looked back, he was standing on the terrace waving and pointing to the book in his hand, as if to remind me of what we'd said to each other.

I walked on a little farther, and when I looked back once more, he was gone.

CHAPTER 27

THE SEA MONSTER

Deep night had come to the Lonely Sea during the telling of Roland's tale. My emotions were frayed like a sail that had been battered by a driving wind, and I was tired and sore from sitting so long on the wooden deck. Yipes seemed to feel none of my discomforts as he began the expected inquisition into the details of the story he'd just been told.

"I was willing to wait until the very end," he said with a teasing dignity, "but now you *must* tell us about this place — the Five Stone Pillars — and what became of Sir Alistair Wakefield and all the lost children. Surely you can tell us that much!"

There was real panic in his voice now, as if he feared being denied the knowledge he'd so patiently waited for. I rose to my feet and stretched loudly, knowing full well that the very best result Yipes could hope for would be an answer that would come after a torturously long pause from Roland at the wheel.

"Trust me this once," said Roland, and I knew something difficult was coming. "You'll need your rest come morning. Let's all lie here together, with the blankets around us and the few pillows we have, and get a few hours of sleep. Then I'll be happy to tell you about the Five Stone Pillars."

Yipes protested vigorously at first, and even I complained of wanting more, but looking at Roland in the little light from the candles, I saw that he was utterly exhausted. He lay down on the deck, and we huddled together with the blankets and the pillows, listening to Yipes whine quietly. Soon his protests became a whimper, and then a heavy breathing, and finally a soft snoring in the open air. Then I too fell fast asleep.

When morning came, I turned and saw that Roland was not among the blankets. I roused Yipes with some effort and we scrambled to our feet, sore from sleeping on the hard deck of the boat but anxious to find the captain. He stood off to one side, away from the wheel, gazing out onto the open sea with the spyglass. Approaching him, Yipes hopped up onto the narrow ledge of the rail, and I came alongside. We both stared in the direction Roland was looking, where the early morning sun was beginning to rise up.

"There," Roland said, and for a moment I had a spooky feeling he himself was Sir Alistair Wakefield, come to us from the past to show us which way to go. Roland had his finger pointing across the bow, toward the rising sun.

"Can I please have my spyglass back?" I asked Roland,

276

for there before us — a long ways off — rose the Five Stone Pillars.

"A deal is a deal," answered Roland. "I think I'll keep a hold of it for the moment."

How I wished I could have it back, to peer through its lens and see more clearly the place we approached.

"I can't believe we're here!" cried Yipes.

"And now to your questions," Roland offered. "Which I do agree I owe you answers to. Soon enough you'll get your chance to see all of the Five Stone Pillars, though I must warn you that our approach is complicated and dangerous. It will take some work."

Roland slid the spyglass into his pocket and retreated to the wheel. "There are bridges dangling between the five fingers, and long lines leading down to the water below. A whole society has grown up here. This place has complications and dangers of its own. You'll discover this for yourselves soon enough."

"Will we meet Alistair?" asked Yipes.

"I'm an old man these days," said Roland. "And I'm afraid Sir Alistair Wakefield's time has long since passed."

I had done the math and known that there could be no other answer to the question Yipes had posed. And yet to hear Roland say it — the finality of it — was a little hard to take. I had carried a glimmer of hope that somehow we might meet him.

"So the lost children have grown up?" I asked.

"They have indeed."

"What will we find up there? On the Five Stone Pillars?" Yipes remained on the rail, perched there like a cat.

"Some things you wouldn't expect," Roland answered.

This sort of answer drove Yipes mad with curiosity. He bound off the rail, ran across the deck, and bunched Roland's pant legs in his tiny hands.

"Why must you torture me so?"

Roland laughed the kind of hearty laugh you might expect from a weathered man of the sea.

"I'm sorry, old friend, I just can't tell you. You'll have to see it for yourself."

Yipes let go of Roland's pants and slumped down on the deck. I came away from the rail and sat down, putting my arm around him.

"There's one thing more I must tell you," Roland continued. "I feel you deserve to know, though it is an unfortunate bit of bad news if you happen to be a group of friends sailing on the open water."

Yipes perked up, and we both rose back onto our feet together.

"Go ahead," said Yipes. "We can take it."

Roland smiled, but only a little, and then he told us the last of what he had to say before we prepared to make our approach to the Five Stone Pillars.

"You remember what happened before — when Grindall and the ogres were finally defeated and they fell into the pit?"

"You mean the terrible noise?"

Roland shook his head. "Not that. Do you recall how a part of The Land of Elyon broke off and slid into the Lonely Sea?"

I remembered. It was a monstrous feeling, like a rolling earthquake. Like the whole Land of Elyon was coming apart.

"After that — when we were home in Lathbury for a time — do you remember when I went off on my own and was away for a while?"

"I *do* remember that," said Yipes. "We looked for you. We kept checking the boat, thinking you were going to leave without us."

"I followed an old path."

"A path to where?" I asked.

"Into the Great Ravine, through a secret cave, and past an iron door."

"You didn't!" said Yipes.

"I wanted to see something for myself, something that had been troubling me."

Roland looked out toward the Five Stone Pillars and turned the wheel back a half turn to the left. He seemed to be trying very hard to make our approach along a certain line in his memory.

"I went the way Thomas and I had gone, but when I got to the middle on the raft I let the current carry me where it would. It was dim for a long time, but then the Lake of Fire seemed to shimmer as it hadn't before. I rounded a corner with high stone walls, and the light grew brighter. Soon I came to a place where I saw what I'd hoped I wouldn't see."

"An opening," I whispered. A fierce chill ran through me as I began to put together what Roland was trying to tell us.

"A very big opening to the outside, to the rolling water of the Lonely Sea."

Yipes — for all his curiosity and desire to know the truth — seemed perplexed or unwilling to know the truth. Roland spun the wheel to the right once more, then came down on one knee and looked at Yipes and me.

"Abaddon is loose on the water — a sea monster of unspeakable cruelty and power."

He stood up and took charge of the wheel. "An ancient evil roams these waters just as we do, searching for something."

"For what?" asked Yipes, his voice soft and shaking.

"For a new place to call home."

I looked off toward the Five Stone Pillars.

"Why did you bring us here?" I asked.

There was a long silence from our captain. I leaned over the rail and searched the sea for the slightest sign of a dark, moving shadow beneath the water.

"To save them from the coming monster," he finally said. "To bring them back home, if only we can."

I looked up once more at the strange sight of the Five Stone Pillars growing closer, and heard a chill in Roland's voice as he gave a final word.

"We have arrived in the realm of lost children."

To be continued . . .

Join Alexa's journey to confront Elyon's dark forces...and her destiny.

The LAND of ELYON

Patrick Carman's *New York Times* bestselling series